S0-BBP-865

"This is insane."

His lips pressed against her throat. "You wanted me to make love to you last night, and you were afraid."

"Don't be ridiculous. I never—"

"I asked you a question last night, Francesca. And you answered it. Can you recall?"

She drew a deep breath. "No. I—I don't remember."

A tight smile curved across his mouth. "Then I must refresh your memory."

SANDRA MARTON says she has always believed in the magic of storytelling and the joy of living happily ever after with that special someone. She wrote her first romance story when she was nine, seven years before she fell madly in love at the age of sixteen with the man she would eventually marry. Today, after raising two sons and an assortment of four-legged creatures, Sandra and her husband live in a house on a hilltop in a quiet corner of Connecticut.

Books by Sandra Marton

HARLEQUIN PRESENTS
1379—CONSENTING ADULTS
1411—GARDEN OF EDEN
1443—BY DREAMS BETRAYED
1457—LOST IN A DREAM
1524—THAT LONG-AGO SUMMER
1574—ROARKE'S KINGDOM

Don't miss any of our special offers. Write to us at the following address for information on our newest releases.

Harlequin Reader Service
P.O. Box 1397, Buffalo, NY 14240
Canadian address: P.O. Box 603,
Fort Erie, Ont. L2A 5X3

SANDRA MARTON

The Corsican Gambit

Harlequin Books

TORONTO • NEW YORK • LONDON
AMSTERDAM • PARIS • SYDNEY • HAMBURG
STOCKHOLM • ATHENS • TOKYO • MILAN
MADRID • WARSAW • BUDAPEST • AUCKLAND

If you purchased this book without a cover you should be aware
that this book is stolen property. It was reported as "unsold and
destroyed" to the publisher, and neither the author nor the
publisher has received any payment for this "stripped book."

ISBN 0-373-11637-3

THE CORSICAN GAMBIT

Copyright © 1991 by Sandra Myles.

All rights reserved. Except for use in any review, the reproduction or
utilization of this work in whole or in part in any form by any electronic,
mechanical or other means, now known or hereafter invented, including
xerography, photocopying and recording, or in any information storage
or retrieval system, is forbidden without the written permission of the
publisher, Harlequin Enterprises Limited, 225 Duncan Mill Road,
Don Mills, Ontario, Canada M3B 3K9.

All characters in this book have no existence outside the imagination of
the author and have no relation whatsoever to anyone bearing the same
name or names. They are not even distantly inspired by any individual
known or unknown to the author, and all incidents are pure invention.

This edition published by arrangement with Harlequin Enterprises B. V.

® and TM are trademarks of the publisher. Trademarks indicated with
® are registered in the United States Patent and Trademark Office, the
Canadian Trade Marks Office and in other countries.

Printed in U.S.A.

CHAPTER ONE

SHE'D ALMOST been too late. Charles had insisted that she join him at the Café de Paris for drinks with a fat little man whose name and title had been meant to impress.

She'd stayed the minimum time that convention required, then begged off, murmuring apologies despite the look of disapproval on her stepbrother's handsome face.

"Forgive me," she'd said, pushing back her chair, "but I've—I've got an appointment."

A smile curved across Francesca's mouth. It hadn't been a lie, not in the strict sense of the word. This *was* an appointment, a far more pleasurable one than the game of "Can You Match This?" that Charles and the fat man had been playing with their seemingly casual talk of Bentleys and Rolexes and out-of-the-way luxury vacation spots. But that sort of thing wasn't for her. She much preferred sitting here, in their hotel suite, watching the sun expand into an enormous crimson fireball that set ablaze the sleek yachts at anchor in the harbor.

It was a spectacular sight—and the least pretentious one she'd seen since arriving in Monaco two days ago, she thought, sighing as the sun began its final plunge behind the hills of France. Not that she didn't like the tiny principality: its narrow, winding streets had an old-world charm, despite the high-rise apartment buildings that crowded on Monte Carlo.

It was just that she'd never seen so much expensive artifice in all her twenty-three years. Everything seemed to spell "excess," from the gilt cherubs that adorned the ceilings of the Casino to the jewels that glittered at the throats and fingers of the stylishly dressed women who

drifted from Bulgari to Cartier to Piaget along the
Avenue des Beaux Arts. Charles disagreed. "Not
excess," he'd said that morning when she'd demurred
at spending an outrageous sum of money on a silk catsuit
that had caught her eye. "It's success, Francesca. The
look of affluence." And then he'd motioned to the shop
assistant to wrap the jumpsuit and put it on his charge
account. "Just relax and enjoy yourself, darling. That's
why I brought you along."

Francesca sighed as she stepped back into the room.
Yes, she thought, that was what he'd said when he'd
first asked her to come to the conference of international financial advisers with him. But she'd gone on
a couple of these junkets before; experience had made
her wary.

"I can't," she'd said, offering the first excuse she could
think of. "I'm needed at the gallery."

Charles had touched her hair, the way he'd used to
when they were little.

"I'm sure you're a wonderful assistant, darling, but
I hardly think they'd deny you a holiday."

Francesca had looked him straight in the eye. "Will
it be a holiday, really? Or will it be lots of cocktail parties
and banquets where everyone tries to impress the hell
out of everyone else?"

Charles had laughed and given her the smile that had
been able to melt her since she'd first seen it, when she
was eight and he seventeen.

"We'll have a good time, I promise. Do say you'll
come with me—you've never been to the Riviera. It'll
be fun."

Eventually she'd agreed. The trip *had* sounded like
fun: Charles had talked about the sea and the sun and
the wonderful little towns that stretched between Cannes
and Monaco until Francesca could almost envisage them.
She'd dreamed of spending lazy days on the beach, the
silken glide of a warm sea, and long hours in which to
do nothing but strengthen the bonds between herself and

her stepbrother. They'd been close as children, but lately they seemed to have drifted apart.

Francesca grimaced as she unzipped her Lagerfeld linen dress and slipped it from her shoulders. She should have known what she was letting herself in for when Charles had suddenly urged her to buy herself some new things at Saks, but by then all the arrangements had been made. And now, here she was, shuttling from luncheon to tea to cocktail party to dinner, smiling on cue and trying her best to be what Charles teasingly called Spencer Investment's secret weapon.

"You're the firm's best asset," he kept saying. "Let me show you off." And, when she'd protested that she didn't feel comfortable being shown off, Charles had sighed. "I know, darling. But you can smile and in one evening win us business it might normally take me a year of hard work to gain."

How could she protest when she owed him so much? He had taken care of her in the years since their parents' death in a plane crash and had been as kind and thoughtful as any big brother, even if they weren't related by blood. He'd offered no complaint in taking on the burden of managing Spencer's alone when she'd shown an interest in art, not economics.

And Charles had done well. The family-owned firm had been prosperous long before she and he had inherited equal shares of its controlling stock, but lately its success had been almost phenomenal. Charles was too modest to tell her much about what he'd done; she knew only that he'd come up with a series of brilliant and innovative investment strategies that had moved Spencer's ahead of its competitors.

For a man who'd had to repeat virtually every mathematics and economics course he'd taken at university, it was quite a turnaround, and Francesca was proud of him. If she could help, even a little, by dressing up and smiling politely and meeting the other conference attendees, well, she would grit her teeth and do it.

But not tonight. Tonight, their next to last in Monaco, was hers and hers alone. She would wear no couture gowns, no jewels, no carefully applied makeup. She wouldn't dine on lobster at La Coupole, or on caviar and champagne at Louis XV.

Francesca smiled as she kicked off her shoes and dress, then pulled on a pair of white cotton pants and a matching knitted top. Her fingers flew as she pulled back her shoulder-length wheaten hair and twisted it into a French braid. Tonight, they were going to do all the things she'd been longing to do for the past two days. First a brisk walk to the top of Tête de Chien to see the view, then pizza at Pinocchio's. Just picturing Charles eating pizza was enough to make her smile become a grin.

She plucked a pair of sandals from the cupboard and slipped her feet into them. After supper, she was going to try and talk him into driving their rented Mercedes to Juan-les-Pins, or Nice. Francesca laughed softly. Actually, she was almost hoping Charles might refuse. Then she could take the car out herself and try driving *la grande corniche*, the legendary, breathtaking road between Monaco and Nice...

"Francesca?"

She looked up, startled. The bedroom door swung open and Charles stepped into the room, his face illuminated by the moonlight coming through the open balcony door.

"What are you doing in the dark?" he said. "Are you all right?"

"Yes, of course. I'm fine."

"First you run off that way and now I find you moping around in the dark."

"The moonlight suits my mood, Charles." She heard the click of the switch and she blinked in the sudden glare of light that flooded the room. "Hey," she said lightly, "what are you trying to do? Blind me?"

Charles's brows rose. "Is that what you're wearing to the Marquesa's party, darling?" He laughed pleasantly. "I hardly think it will go with my tuxedo."

Francesca's face fell. "What party? Charles, you promised I could have tonight to myself."

"Yes, I know. But we've only just been asked." He walked to her cupboard and peered into it. "I wouldn't go, normally, not with such a last-minute invitation. But that whole Madrid bunch will be there, the ones I've had such difficulty doing business with."

"Well, you won't need me along, will you? I mean, it will be a big party, with lots and lots of people."

"Where's that gold thing you wore the night of my birthday last month? Didn't you bring it with you?"

"Charles, you're not listening to me. I'm not much for parties, you know that."

"Ah, here it is." He turned to her, smiling, holding out the glittering gown. "The Marquesa especially mentioned you, Francesca. She said she looked forward to seeing you again." When she said nothing, he sighed. "But I suppose I can always offer your apologies."

Francesca stared at his crestfallen face. "Does my going really matter so much?" she asked slowly, watching him.

He shrugged. "You know how it is, darling. See and be seen, that's what it's all about. But if you don't want to——"

She sighed. "Give me half an hour," she said, kicking off the sandals.

Charles smiled and dropped a kiss on the top of her head as he made for the door.

"Thank you, darling. I'll make it up to you, I promise."

"Yes, you will." Francesca smiled, too. "You'll spend all of tomorrow with me, doing whatever I like."

His smile grew tight. "I'm not exactly dragging you off to purgatory, you know."

"Aren't you?" She laughed. "Well, we'll just wait and see."

Two hours later, wearing the slim gold gown as Charles had requested, her hair twisted into a soft knot atop her head, Francesca had decided that if this wasn't purgatory, it was awfully close to it. For one thing, it didn't seem to be the Marquesa who'd been looking forward to seeing her; it was the Marqués. He gave her a wet kiss that would have landed on her lips if she hadn't turned her head in time, then looped a soft, beefy arm around her waist and spent the next twenty minutes breathing gin in her face while he twirled her around the crowded dance floor.

She was saved by the Marquesa, who dragged her off on a tour of what she called her "cottage." The humble designation was almost ludicrous. The "cottage" was, in reality, an enormous stucco structure with vine-covered walls, a red-tiled roof, formal gardens, and a breathtaking view of the sea far below.

And yet, as big as the house was, it was almost impossible to draw a breath of air. The rooms were jammed with heavily laden tables of food, trays of drinks, and clots of people straining to make themselves heard over the bands.

"Two," the Marquesa bubbled, "one for the—how you say?—the rock. And one for the other kind, the cheek to cheek."

As it turned out, both were a waste. By eleven o'clock both dance floors, located at either end of the huge house, were so crowded that no one could move a foot, let alone dance, even though Charles kept urging her out on the floor each time someone invited her.

"Go on, darling, have a good time," he kept saying.

She tried. But the men were the same sort that she knew from New York and the fact that they were here, on the Riviera, didn't make them any more interesting. She didn't like the way they talked, dropped names as if they were crumbs, or the way they all smelled of the latest designer cologne, and she especially didn't like the way some of them tried to hold her.

"Having fun?" Charles kept saying.

He was, by the looks of him. When the Marqués reappeared and put a hand on each of their shoulders, Charles fairly beamed.

"You will join me at midnight for supper."

It was a statement, not a question, but Francesca smiled pleasantly and said she wasn't really very hungry.

Charles smiled at her, but she could see that he was annoyed.

"My sister's forever dieting," he lied. "But I'm sure she's not going to pass up all that delectable food. We'd be delighted to join you, my lord."

The Marqués slapped him on the back. "Good. Let's have a chat first, shall we? I'd like to hear more about those investment opportunities of yours."

Francesca let out her breath as the two men headed away from her. She was going to have to have a talk with Charles tomorrow. It was one thing to be polite, but it was quite another to—to make her feel as if she were being offered up for barter. Certainly, that wasn't her stepbrother's intention, but it was how he'd made her feel. Once she made Charles aware of it...

"Hello." She looked up. A young man whose name she didn't recall was smiling at her, a flute of champagne in his outstretched hand. "I thought you looked thirsty, so I came on a mission of mercy."

Francesca took the wine and sipped at it as he launched into a discussion of the difference between the beaches on the Riviera and those in South America. He seemed determined to compare every grain of sand he'd ever seen. She smiled as best she could, hoping she wouldn't yawn—and then, suddenly, she felt a curious sensation, sort of a tingling along her spine.

Someone was watching her. She knew it; she could feel his eyes on her. She blinked and tried to concentrate on what the boy beside her was saying. Something about the beaches in the Bahamas, and—and——

The strange feeling came again. But it was silly. How could she *feel* someone looking at her? Besides, it was impossible. In a room this crowded, you'd never be able to look at anyone except the person right next to you.

Still, the idea that she was being watched persisted.

Francesca turned slowly, as if she were only shifting position, and scanned the crowded room surreptitiously—and yes, there *was* someone watching her, a man. She had never seen him before. She knew that immediately. He was not the kind of man who would be easily forgotten. He was dressed no differently from many of the other men, in a white dinner jacket. He even wore a ruffled shirt, as did the others. But the softness of the shirt only emphasized the hardness of his tanned, strong-jawed face, and the tailored jacket made the most of his broad shoulders, hinting at a lean and powerful body.

There was a woman with him, a stunning brunette in a creamy satin gown. Her hand lay possessively on his arm, her lovely face was turned up to his. But he wasn't paying her any attention; he was looking beyond her to Francesca through eyes that seemed blue, or perhaps black. Yes. Black. As black as the night, as black as the sky would be if all the stars were gone.

Her breath caught as their glances met. She wanted to look away, but his eyes held hers for what seemed an eternity, and then a slow, cool smile curved across his mouth. His gaze fell, moved down her body with slow deliberation before returning just as slowly to her face. His smile changed, grew private, and sent a message racing through her blood. Francesca felt her heartbeat quicken; color rose under her skin and flooded her face.

Suddenly, the brunette turned, her gaze following his. She stared at Francesca, her lovely face hardening, and then she swung in front of the man, grasped his wrist and pulled him toward the dance floor. The crowd surged around them, swallowing them up, and Francesca suddenly realized she had not drawn a breath since the moment she had first seen him.

Her hand trembled as she put down her glass.

"Will you excuse me?" she said politely, and before the young man beside her could answer she slipped past him and made her way to the door.

The terrace was only a little less crowded than the house, but at least the air wasn't as thick. Francesca stood still for several seconds, taking deep breaths, and then she gave a little laugh. Maybe Charles was right and she needed to eat something. She was light-headed, she had to be. It was the only way to explain that nonsense just now.

Francesca made her way briskly toward the wide brick steps that led down into the gardens surrounding the house. Who wouldn't be light-headed after trying to breath perfume and cigarette smoke for two hours? A walk would clear the cobwebs.

The gardens had been terraced to take best advantage of the steep slope. A narrow path zigzagged through flowering shrubs and heavily laden rosebushes, and soon she was far from the noisy confusion of the party. Her steps slowed. This solitary walk had been a good idea. And—it *was* solitary, wasn't it? For an instant, she'd felt as if she was being followed—followed by the man she'd seen across the room.

Her heartbeat skidded at the thought. She paused, lifted and half turned her head, listening, trying to sense his presence. The thought of him coming after her was—was...

Francesca laughed softly. Yes, she thought, coming to the stone wall that marked the path's end, she was most definitely light-headed. What she'd do, when she got back to the house, was head for the buffet table. Unless, by some stroke of good fortune, Charles had finished his business with the Marqués and they could——

"They say you can see Italy from here."

She whirled around. It was him, the man who'd been watching her earlier. He was standing an arm's length away, his body blocking the narrow path.

"What are you doing here?" she said.

He smiled. "Enjoying the view, the same as you. Do you object?"

A flush rose in her cheeks. "It's a public garden."

His smile broadened. "Really? I think the Marquesa would be distressed to hear that."

"I didn't mean it that way, exactly. I meant..." Her flush deepened. Ridiculous, to be this tongue-tied. And even more ridiculous to stand here and play this stranger's game. She drew herself up. "Excuse me."

His brows rose. "Yes?"

Francesca gave him her coolest look. "Would you mind stepping aside? I'd like to get by."

He stepped forward into a pool of moonlight. "But you haven't even taken a look at those mountains," he said softly. "They're the Maritime Alps. They mark the Italian border."

"Really?" Her tone was as cool as her expression. "I have a better view than this from my hotel room. Now, if you'd please——"

He reached out as she started to sweep past him, his hand closing lightly on her bare arm, his fingers cool on her skin.

"You *wanted* me to follow you." His voice was low-pitched and firm with conviction. "I watched you. You turned and searched for me."

Color raced into her cheeks. "I did no such thing."

His eyes were as black as a bottomless pool as they swept across her face.

"Didn't you?" he asked softly.

Suddenly, she wanted to tear free of his hand and run for the lighted safety of the house. But the light touch of his fingers on her arm imprisoned her, as surely as if it were a manacle of steel.

"You flatter yourself." Her voice was calm, cool with contempt despite the racing beat of her heart. "And now, if you'd be good enough to let go of me——"

He laughed. "I'll bet that's never failed you yet, has it? That regal bearing, the frigid tone."

"You're talking nonsense."

"Hell, it probably brings them to their knees each time." His teeth flashed in the darkness. "Don't you feel any guilt for what you did to all those young men?"

Francesca twisted against his hand. "Will you let go of me?" she said furiously.

"I have to admit, it was fascinating to watch you. Playing with those poor boys, letting them kneel at your feet." His smile changed, grew as intimate as the one he'd given her when she'd first looked into his eyes. "Is it all a game, *bellissima*?" His hand slid to her wrist and tightened on the fragile bones. "Or is it only that no man has ever made you want him?"

A tremor raced along her flesh. "If you don't let go of me this second," she said, "I'll—I'll——"

His laughter cut across her careful speech. "You'll what? Scream?"

"Yes." Her voice shook. "I will. I'll scream and scream..."

"Go on, then," he whispered. His arm slid around her and he drew her to him, while his free hand slid up her throat and cupped her chin, tilting her head back until her mouth was turned up to his. "Scream, if that's really what you want to do." His thumb moved slowly across her lips. "But first kiss me, kiss me with your mouth as you did with your eyes when you looked at me tonight. And then—then tell me you want to leave."

Her breath hissed raggedly from between parted lips. "You're crazy," she whispered.

He smiled. "Am I?" he said, and his mouth came down on hers.

Francesca went still at the first touch of his lips, telling herself that he would let her go if she offered no reaction. Later, when she was safe in her hotel room, when the moon and the stars were once again steady in the firmament, she would wonder if it was that initial stillness that had doomed her.

If she'd fought him, perhaps his kiss wouldn't have become so seductive. Perhaps he wouldn't have moved his mouth over hers as he did, teasing her, urging her to open to him. Perhaps he wouldn't have moved his tongue lightly along her barely parted lips until she felt as if she were being touched by a flame.

Something dark stirred deep within Francesca's soul, and she began to tremble. A sound whispered from her throat, so soft it seemed almost lost in the encompassing night. But he heard it, understood it, and he gathered her to him, his hand sweeping down her spine and molding her body to his.

"Yes," he said fiercely, "yes."

The triumph in his voice carried through her like an electric charge. She felt herself explode like sheet lightning. Her mouth parted, her hands lifted; she caught his shirt in her fingers, rose on her toes, pressed closer to him.

His groan was primitive and elementally male. "I wanted to do this the minute I saw you," he whispered. Her head fell back as his lips trailed a fiery path down her throat; she felt him pluck the pins from her hair, felt it tumble to her shoulders. He thrust his hands into it and brought her face to his. *"Bellissima,"* he said in an urgent whisper. "You are so beautiful."

God, what was happening to her? She was drowning, drowning in a sea far warmer than the one that beat at the rocks far below. Her hands rose again and linked behind his neck. His hair was thick, silken to the touch. Her eyes closed as his mouth moved against her skin. What would it be like to feel his naked body against hers? Would his skin be hot, like his mouth? His body would be hard; it would press her down into the softness of his bed.

Noises drifted through the garden toward the dark corner where they stood locked together. The crunch of gravel, the tinkle of laughter...

Francesca stiffened in the man's arms. Sanity returned quickly, along with the fear of discovery.

"Let go of me!" He raised his head slowly, his eyes blurred with arousal as they focused on her face. "Dammit," she hissed, pushing against his chest, "didn't you hear me? Someone's coming."

His hand closed around her wrist. "My car is just outside." There was urgency in his voice. "We can be in Nice in half an hour."

"No. Are you crazy? I can't——"

"Paris, then. Rome." He pulled her off the path, into the shadow of a palm tree and kissed her until she was breathless. "I know a hill above the city where the starlight falls on an ancient circle of stones." His hand moved over her, laying possessive claim to her flesh. "Let me make love to you there, *inamorata*, with only the moon to see."

She felt herself waver. But the footsteps were closer now, and suddenly she saw herself as others would see her, as *he* must see her, a woman lost in the arms of a man she had never seen before, a man whose name she didn't even know.

She turned, whirling out of his arms just as a group of laughing guests appeared on the path.

"Whoops," a voice called in a slurred giggle, "what have we here?"

People fell back, laughing, as Francesca pushed her way past them. She heard a peal of drunken laughter, then an angry voice she knew must be his, but by then she was flying toward the lighted safety of the house.

Charles was waiting at the terrace steps. "Where in hell have you been?" he demanded, his voice low and tight with anger. "The Marqués looked everywhere." He stepped back and stared at her. "What happened?" he said. "Just look at you, Francesca. You look—you look..."

She flushed as he looked at her. She could imagine how she appeared, with her hair undone and her flushed face. But there was no way to explain, not without humiliating herself. Instead, she forced herself to meet Charles's stare calmly.

"I'm going back to the hotel, Charles."

If she'd thought he was going to question her, she was wrong.

"Yes," he said, "but the Marqués——"

Her head came up. "To hell with the Marqués," she said, her voice trembling.

Her stepbrother looked as if she'd struck him. "Shh," he said, waving his hand and glancing back at the house.

Francesca spun on her heel and started marching towards the narrow road that wound down the steep hillside.

"I'll take the car," she said over her shoulder. "You can phone for a taxi."

There was a moment's silence, and then Charles uttered a sharp oath and fell into place beside her.

"What the hell's gotten into you tonight?" he grumbled.

It was, she thought unhappily, a damned good question.

CHAPTER TWO

FRANCESCA opened her bedroom door quietly, then peered into the sitting room of the suite she and her step-brother shared. Charles was already seated at the breakfast table, buttering a croissant as he frowned over his copy of the *International Herald Tribune*.

She drew back. The desire to close the door and stay hidden behind it until he left the room was almost overwhelming, but what would that gain her? She'd have to see him, sooner or later, and anticipating the moment would only make it worse.

Last night, Charles had honored her silence. Francesca made a face. That wasn't really accurate. The truth was, his anger at her had made him sullen. It was a trait he'd always had. Usually, she responded to his sulky stillness by trying to joke him out of it.

But last evening she'd taken advantage of it. She hadn't said a word to him after they'd left the party, nothing except a quickly murmured "good night" after they reached their suite, and then she'd gone into her room, shut the door, and tried to make sense out of what had happened in the Marqués's garden.

She sighed. She had never, in all her life, behaved that way before. There was just no explanation for it. The man was good-looking, yes, but she knew lots of good-looking men. They were a staple of the New York social scene. It was true that not all of them—perhaps *none* of them—had quite the same air of blatant masculinity as the stranger, but so what? She wasn't a teenage girl, so starry-eyed that she swooned when a sexy man came on to her.

And that was certainly what he'd done. All that stuff about the way he'd felt the moment he'd first looked at her...

Francesca closed her eyes in disgust. That line was so old it creaked!

So if all that were true—and she knew it was—then why had she fallen into his arms? Heat flared beneath her skin. Why had she melted at his touch? She didn't even know his name...

"Is it only that no man has ever made you want him?"

Her eyes flew open. His voice was inside her head, but it was so real that it seemed, for an instant, in the room with her. She would never forget the sound of it, deep and very definitely American, despite all the *caras* and *bellissimas*.

"Francesca? Is that you, darling?"

Charles was calling her. Time to face the music, she thought. She took a deep breath, then glanced into the mirror. Her face was paler than usual, but other than that she looked herself.

"Francesca?"

Take another breath. Now smile...

"Yes," she called, and she stepped briskly into the sitting room, as if this day were no different than any other.

Charles looked up. "Good morning."

"Good morning." She bent and kissed his cheek. "Mmm, the coffee smells wonderful. Just what I need."

She sank into the chair opposite his. Charles looked at her, then reached for the pots of coffee and hot milk that stood on the serving cart.

"Shall I pour?"

"Please." She watched as he tilted the pots and poured twin streams of steaming white and black into her over-size breakfast cup. "Perfect café au lait," she said, smiling. "You've learned to do that very well in the past days."

Her stepbrother offered her the basket of warm croissants and brioches.

"You know what they say," he said pleasantly, "when in Rome . . ." He fell silent, watching as Francesca broke off a piece of croissant and spread it with raspberry jam. "Well, now. What shall we do today?"

It was all she could do to keep from breathing a sigh of relief. No questions. Thank goodness. Because she certainly had no answers.

"That is, if you're free."

She smiled as she put down her butter knife. "Of course I'm free. You know that. Today's our last day — we said we'd go see the Oceanographic Institute, remember?"

Charles put his elbows on the table, folded his hands, and steepled his fingers beneath his chin.

"Yes, so we did." His eyes were cool. "I thought perhaps you'd made other plans."

"Other plans? What do you mean?"

He shrugged. "You tell me."

There was a faintly taunting quality to his voice. Francesca stirred uneasily.

"How can I," she said, "when I don't know what you're talking about?"

An unpleasant little smile caught at the corner of his mouth. "It occurred to me that you might have made arrangements to meet your friend."

"My . . . ?" She swallowed. "What do you mean?"

"I was referring to the man you had that romantic little tryst with last night."

Two crimson circles flamed in her cheeks.

"That's unkind. I didn't *tryst* with anyone," she said.

"Please, Francesca." Her stepbrother sat back and folded his arms across his chest. "I'm not an idiot."

She drew a deep breath. "Charles——"

His voice was cold. "There's no point in trying to deny it. I saw the way you looked."

"All right. I was—I was with someone. But not the way you——"

"How could you?" Charles shoved back his chair and got to his feet. "How could you have behaved so badly?"

Francesca looked at him. "You have no right to speak to me that way," she said quietly.

His mouth thinned. "Haven't I?"

"What I did was—it was foolish. But I'm not a child, Charles. I don't have to ask your permission before I..." She hesitated, and then she looked down into the milky liquid in her cup. "Look," she said, her voice low, "I can't explain what happened. It was just—it was crazy, I know. But——"

"There I was," Charles said through his teeth, "offering one ridiculous excuse after another to the Marqués. Perhaps she stepped out for some air, I said. Perhaps she's indisposed, I said. Perhaps she's in another part of the house, talking to someone, I said." He clasped the back of the chair next to hers and bent toward her, his face dark. "And all the time, you were out there in the dark, playing catch-me-if-you-can with some man."

Color sprang into her cheeks again, but her eyes were steady on his.

"I don't think much of your choice of words," she said evenly.

"And I don't think much of your loyalties. You *knew* you were supposed to have supper with the Marqués." Charles straightened, then marched to the window. "You heard me assure him that you would. But did that matter to you?" he demanded, spinning toward her. "No, it did not. You went off and——"

"Is that what this is all about?" She stared at him. "You're upset because I didn't keep a promise you made on my behalf?"

His mouth narrowed. "Do you have any idea how much money the Marqués has invested with Spencer's, my dear sister? Better still, do you have the foggiest notion how much he's *thinking* of investing?"

Francesca gave a little laugh. "I don't believe this. Here I was, thinking you were concerned about me, and all the time, it was your precious Marqués you were worried about."

"He's not *my* Marqués, sister dear, he's ours. He's a client, don't you understand? And he deserves proper treatment."

"Meaning me at his side during supper?" She shook her head as she pushed back her chair. "Thanks, but no, thanks. I don't like playing that kind of game."

"Being hospitable is part of doing business."

"I've no quarrel with that," she said as she got to her feet. "But I don't like the way you—you dangle me in front of people sometimes."

Charles blew out his breath. "That's ridiculous. I've told you, you're an asset for the company."

"Which makes no sense at all. I don't have anything to do with Spencer's."

Her stepbrother looked at her. "But you do, Francesca." He smiled tightly. "You own half the controlling stock, remember?"

"Yes. And you always vote it for me."

His face flushed. "Are you complaining about the decisions I've made for the firm?"

"No. Of course not. I just——"

"I've always tried to do the best job possible. I should think you'd know that better than anyone."

"I do, Charles. I only meant——"

His mouth turned down. "Spencer's had to be pushed into the twentieth century after our parents' death."

"I know that, too," she said quickly. The anger had fled his face, leaving behind a look of unhappiness that cut into her heart. "You've worked hard, Charles. And you've done a fine job."

He nodded stiffly. "God knows I've tried, though it hasn't always been easy."

"No," she said softly, "I'm sure it hasn't been. You had so much thrust on you——"

He shrugged and turned away from her. "There wasn't any choice."

Francesca caught her lip between her teeth. It was true, she thought, watching his tensed shoulders, life had asked a great deal of her stepbrother. Augustus Spencer had married her mother when Francesca was eight and Charles seventeen. Nine years later, when their parents' plane had crashed against a Colorado mountain peak, Charles had suddenly had to assume the responsibility for running the investment firm his father had founded and the responsibility of raising her, as well.

He had done it all with no complaints, asking nothing in return until recently, when she'd finished her art courses at university, and then it had been only that she occasionally play hostess or accompany him to an important social event.

Francesca felt a stab of conscience. It was little enough to do for the man who'd been father, brother, and provider for the past six years.

Having supper with the Marqués last night certainly wouldn't have killed her.

She sighed. Charles was still standing at the window, his back to her. She called his name softly.

"Charles?"

"What?"

She walked to his side and put her hand on his arm. "I—I didn't mean to let you down last night."

There was a silence, and then he sighed, too. "And I didn't mean to jump down your throat."

"I just didn't like the way the Marqués kept after me."

Charles turned to her. "He likes you, darling. There's nothing wrong with that, is there?"

"I suppose not. It's just that there was something in the way he looked at me..."

He smiled. "Silly girl. I told you, he's fond of you, that's all. He has a granddaughter about your age."

Francesca laughed a little. "The way he looked at me didn't seem terribly paternal."

"I'm sure you read him wrong. He's really a very nice old man."

She sighed. "In that case, I'm doubly sorry I disappointed you."

"If you really mean that——"

"You know I do."

Charles put his arm around her shoulders. "Well, then, we can make our apologies this evening. The Marqués asked us to join him at the Casino. He said he'd look forward to having you beside him as a good-luck charm."

Francesca's stomach clenched. "Must we?"

Something flashed in his eyes—anger, she thought, or even rage—but it was gone so quickly she told herself she'd imagined it.

"No," he said smoothly, "of course not. I'll phone and send our regrets."

"You're sure it's not a problem?"

"Don't worry about it, darling." He gave her a smile, but now she could see that what she'd glimpsed in his eyes was disappointment. "I don't want you to do anything that makes you uncomfortable. The old boy probably won't miss us. I think he invited half of last night's guests to join him this evening."

"We wouldn't be his only guests, you mean?"

Charles shook his head as he reached for the phone. "No, not hardly."

"Well, then . . ." She puffed out her breath. "Let it go." He turned an inquiring glance toward her, and she smiled. "We'll join the Marqués, just as you planned." Her smile widened. "I don't know if I'll bring him good luck, but the Casino should be fun."

"Thank you, darling." Her stepbrother kissed her forehead. "Now, let me just make a couple of quick phone calls and we'll be on our way."

It was only after he'd left the room that Francesca realized that if half of last night's guests were going to

join the Marqués at the Casino one of them might well
be the man she'd encountered in the garden last night.

The possibility was enough to send a shiver of alarm
racing to her nerve endings. She had absolutely no wish
to see him again, ever.

Her chin lifted. But she wasn't going to hide in her
room in the hope of avoiding him, either. He had helped
her make a fool of herself, but what had happened was
over and done.

The sooner she put the whole nonsensical incident
behind her, the better.

The day passed quickly. Charles was perfect company,
as charming and as attentive as he could be when he
wished, ushering her first to the Oceanographic Institute,
where they gaped at huge octopuses and gasped at tanks
filled with colorful Pacific fishes, and then to the Jardin
Exotique which boasted succulents and cacti that equaled
any Francesca had seen in the American southwest. They
toured the cool, cliffside cave that still bore the imprint
of the coast's prehistoric inhabitants, then had a late
lunch of salade niçoise at a noisy, pleasant café near the
Hôtel Hermitage.

Charles insisted on strolling the Avenue des Beaux Arts
and window-shopping all the trendy boutiques. He
bought himself a new gold tank watch at Cartier. "The
exchange rate's in our favor," he said, and when
Francesca peered into Dior's and sighed over a silk gown
shaded in all the colors of the sky at sunset, he insisted
she must have it.

"It's perfect for you, darling."

"But it costs a fortune, Charles. And I don't need it."

"Wear it tonight," he said, "for the Marqués, and
we'll write it off as a business deduction."

He said it lightly with a joking smile on his face, but
Francesca was hard-pressed to smile in return. And later
that evening, when she looked into the mirror and saw
how the fall of pink-and-crimson silk clung to her body,

softly molding itself to her breasts and hips, she felt a sudden flush of discomfort.

She reached behind her and started to unzip the gown. She had other gowns in the closet, as pretty as this. What would it matter if she wore one of them, instead?

There was a knock at the door, and it swung open. "Francesca?" Charles smiled at her. "You look lovely," he said. "And you're ready right on schedule."

"Well, actually, I'm not. I was just going to——"

"Ah, I see. You were trying to close that zipper. Well, turn around, darling, and I'll do it for you."

"No. I mean, that's not——"

But it was too late to protest. The zipper slithered closed, and Charles took her by the shoulders and turned her to face him. His pale eyes swept over her, and she had the crazy thought that, for an instant, they glittered like ice.

"Perfect. The Marqués should be delighted."

Francesca laughed uncomfortably. "What?"

"I'm joking, darling," he said, as he put his arm lightly around her waist. "Now, come on. Let's see if we can win everything we've ever wanted tonight."

Monte Carlo, the heart of the tiny principality of Monaco, was the name of both the world-famous Casino and the rocky hill on which it stood. It was a handsome example of *la belle époque*, its towers and decorative facade reflecting the overblown splendor of the final years of the nineteenth century.

This was Francesca's second visit to the Casino, and she liked it no better this time than she had the last.

"Isn't it elegant?" Charles asked in a low voice as he led her into the foyer.

She nodded, although she wasn't sure that was the word she'd have used to describe the place. Everything seemed larger than life, from the nymphs cavorting across the frescoed ceilings to the gilding that gleamed on almost every surface.

Crowds milled around the roulette and baccarat tables, intent on the spin of the wheel, the turn of the card, and the croupier's rake. Voices murmured imprecations to the dice in every language.

Charles paused at none of the gaming tables. He led her, instead, to a *salle privée*. The private room was even more ornate than the main salon, and a very different crowd played at its tables. Francesca recognized some of the faces from the chic magazines that chronicled the lives of international jet set, others from the moneyed strata in which her brother moved in New York. The air of gaiety and excitement was catching, and all at once she was glad they'd come.

"This looks like fun," she said. "What shall we try first?" But Charles wasn't listening. He was peering intently around the room.

"First," he said, frowning, "we find the Marqués."

Francesca's spirits dipped. "Can't we just buy some chips and play? Surely we don't have to——"

"Ah! There he is." Charles put his arm around her waist and drew her forward. "Now remember, darling, treat him nicely."

Charles's assessment proved to be accurate. The Marqués was surrounded by an entourage. But the moment he saw her, his face lit, he held out his hand, and, between the steady pressure of her stepbrother's fingers in the small of her back and the accommodation of the crowd, Francesca was drawn to his side.

"It is good to see you, my dear." There was an unctuous tone to his voice that set Francesca's teeth on edge. "We searched everywhere for you last night, your charming brother and I."

"Did you?" She smiled politely. "Your villa was so crowded—we must have just missed each other."

"Yes, so Charles informed me. Well, I'll have to make certain I keep you at my side all evening, then. We certainly don't want the crowd to separate us again."

Francesca stiffened as his hand slid from her wrist to her elbow, then down again. His fingers closed tightly around hers, but not before she felt the swift brush of his thumb against her palm.

"There's no danger of that," she said quickly. "I'll be with Charles."

The smile slipped from the Marqués's florid face. "You'll be with me, my dear. Surely your brother made that clear."

Her mouth tightened. "I think you must have misunderstood."

"Antonio." A woman beckoned languidly from the baccarat table. "Aren't you going to play?"

"*Sì*, of course." His hand tightened on Francesca's, and he drew her along with him to the gaming table. "I was only collecting my good-luck charm."

Everyone laughed—everyone except Francesca. She looked around for Charles, but her stepbrother had disappeared into the crowd.

"Well?" She blinked. The Marqués was looking at her and smiling. "The cards," he said, nodding to the one lying on the table before him, "what do you think? Shall I hold? Or shall I ask for another?"

"I don't know very much about baccarat..."

He laughed as he looped a beefy arm around her waist. "A beautiful woman doesn't have to know anything except how to charm a man. And I am certain you excel at that."

Francesca stiffened. "Excuse me," she said, "but I must find my..."

Her words drifted to silence. The hair on the nape of her neck rose. She could feel someone's eyes on her.

No, not someone. She knew who she'd see even before she turned. Her heartbeat quickened. It was the man who'd followed her into the garden the night before. He was standing on the far side of the room, leaning against a gilded pillar. He looked relaxed and casual, with his arms crossed against his chest, but there was nothing relaxed about the way he was watching her.

Francesca could feel the heat of his gaze even at this distance.

Time seemed to halt. The sounds that had just seconds ago filled the room—the murmur of the crowd, the discreet calls of the croupiers, the clink of chips—they all faded, leaving behind only the swift thud of her own heart.

A little smile twisted across his face, as if he had heard it, too, and then, suddenly, the crowd shifted and he was gone.

"Maravilloso!" The Marqués's voice was plummy with good humor. "Look at what you have done for me, Francesca," he said.

She blinked and looked down at the table. The croupier was pushing a large stack of chips toward her.

"Mademoiselle," he said politely.

She shook her head. "They're not mine."

The Marqués chuckled as he leaned forward and unlatched her evening purse. "Of course they are," he said, sweeping the chips into its silken depths. "You're the reason I won."

"But I didn't——"

"Nonsense." His arm settled around her again. She could smell the cloying scent of his cologne mixed with the smell of sweat. "Charles was right," he said, smiling into her eyes. "You are adorable."

She felt a flush rise in her cheeks. *"Señor..."*

"One more deal of the cards, and then we'll try the wheel, eh?" His breath fanned her face as he bent and pressed his damp mouth to her cheek. "And then, who knows? The night is young."

He laughed as his hand moved over her hip, then lightly cupped her bottom. It was all done so quickly that it almost might not have happened, except that Francesca's flesh crawled beneath the silk of her gown.

She stepped back as the Marqués leaned toward the table, stepped back again as the croupier began dealing the cards, and then she turned and made her way through the crowd.

Her teeth clamped together as she fell back against the wall. Wait until she found Charles, she thought, just wait until she found him and told him about what a "very nice old man" his pal, the Marqués, really was.

"It isn't easy, is it?"

She spun toward the amused voice. She knew who it was, even before she saw that increasingly familiar, sardonic smile.

"Don't you have anything better to do than to follow me?" she said coldly.

He grinned. "Such a chilly greeting, after all we have been to each other."

"Did you hear what I said?"

"How much did you get from the old boy? It looked pretty good for ten minutes' work."

Francesca's eyes narrowed. "What?" She followed his gaze to her open evening purse and to the shiny chips glinting inside. Her head snapped up. "If you think I wanted him to give me——"

"God knows you earned it."

Color flooded her cheeks. "You don't know what you're talking about," she said, swinging away from him.

"Don't I?" His hand shot out and caught her wrist. "Why didn't you tell me how things were with you and the Marqués last night?"

"Are you crazy? I'm not——"

"Was that why you were so cautious with me?" His grasp tightened. "Or is the sleeping volcano routine part of the game?" His lips drew back from his teeth. "What's that old song, 'Come on, Baby, Light My Fire'?"

Francesca's teeth gritted as she tried to twist free of him. "Get away from me," she spat.

"Don't be silly." He smiled coolly. "Besides, I have an idea."

"I don't know what you're talking about."

"Don't you?" He stepped closer to her. "You're wasting your talent on that disgusting old man."

She felt the blood drain from her face. "What?"

"I don't disgust you, do I." It was a statement, not a question. His eyes met hers, and what had happened between them last night burned in his dark irises like a hot flame. "No," he said softly, "we both know that I do not."

"Let go of me," Francesca said. Her voice sounded breathless, as if she'd been running uphill. "Do you hear me? Let me go, or I'll——"

"What the Marqués doesn't know won't hurt him." He smiled a little at the sudden rise of color in her face. "Hell," he said softly, "after a steady diet of the old boy, you're entitled to an evening's fun."

Her hand twisted in his steely grasp. "You bastard," she whispered, suddenly understanding his meaning, "you—you..."

"That's right, *cara*. Me." His smile vanished, and now she could see only the fire leaping in his midnight eyes. "Me in your bed, instead of the Marqués." He stepped closer to her, until she felt the whisper of his breath against her cheek. "And we won't waste time standing around the Casino, pretending we need the spin of the wheel as a turn-on." His hand moved on her wrist, slipping lower until she felt the feathery brush of his fingers against hers. "All I have to do is look at you," he said thickly, "and I want you so badly I ache."

"Are you crazy? When I tell my——"

"Why not admit the truth? It's the same for you. You want me. You want to feel my mouth on yours, my hands on your skin."

His gaze dropped to her parted lips, then to the swift rise and fall of her breasts.

"Just look at yourself," he whispered. "Your body is answering for you."

She didn't have to look. She could feel what was happening: her treacherous flesh was quickening as he spoke.

"Let go of me," she said, hating the little sound of panic that threaded her voice. "Do you hear me? Let——"

"Francesca."

Charles's voice was like cold steel. Francesca's eyes swept to her stepbrother's face. He had come up beside them suddenly. He was talking to her, but his eyes were on the man standing beside her.

"Charles." The air whooshed from her lungs; relief raced through her so quickly that her legs felt weak. "There you are," she said. "I was just going to——"

"What the hell are you doing with Maximillian Donelli?" he demanded.

"You mean you know this man, Charles? He—he..." Francesca fell silent. Her stepbrother wasn't paying the slightest attention to her, but neither was Maximillian Donelli. The two were, instead, staring at each other with unveiled hatred. She thought suddenly of films she'd seen of two jungle cats facing off.

"Spencer." Donelli's voice was like the strike of a sword on a stone. "I knew you had to be here. But I kept hoping your instinct for self-preservation would keep you from crawling out from under your rock."

A muscle knotted in Charles's cheek. "Go on," he said with a tight smile, "be as glib as you like, if it makes you feel better. It's just too bad that fast mouth of yours can't stop your company from bleeding."

Donelli's lips drew back from his teeth. "Pinning you against that wall and rearranging your face won't stop it, either, but that may not keep me from doing it."

Charles paled beneath his health-club tan, but his smile didn't waver. "I suppose gutter talk's the best one can expect from a man like you." He looked at Francesca. "We're leaving."

She nodded. There were a dozen questions to ask, but she knew better than to ask even one of them now.

"Fine."

Donelli's brows rose. "Leaving?" He looked at her, his mouth quirked in amusement. "Without the Marqués?"

She could feel her face blazing, but she forced herself to meet his insolent smile.

"That's right," she said evenly. "Disappointed?"

"Very. The old man was a bad choice." His smile became fixed as he looked at her stepbrother. "But Charlie here makes him look like a Christmas present. Surely you can do better."

Francesca heard the hiss of her stepbrother's breath. She stepped forward quickly and put her hand on his arm. It was like being swept downstream toward a roaring falls, she thought wildly. Something terrible was coming, and there didn't seem any way to stop it.

"My name is Francesca Drury," she said softly. "Charles is my stepbrother."

She saw surprise and something more register in Maximillian Donelli's face, and then his eyes went blank.

"Really." His voice was without inflection.

"Yes. Really. And now, if you'll excuse us..."

Her hand clamped down on Charles's arm, and she began walking. He fell in stiffly beside her, and she held her breath. It was not over yet; every instinct told her so. The door was getting nearer. Only ten steps more. Nine. Eight. Seven——

"Spencer." Donelli's voice cracked after them like a whip. She felt Charles shudder.

"Don't answer him," she pleaded.

"I must," he said through his teeth. "People are watching."

"Let them. Charles, please."

But he was already turning around. What choice was there for her but to do the same?

"What do you want, Donelli?"

"How would you like to try your hand at the tables?"

Charles blinked. "What the hell are you talking about?"

Donelli shrugged as he strolled toward them, his powerful shoulders moving easily beneath his expensively tailored dinner jacket.

"I thought we might play a friendly little game of poker." His voice was lazy, almost dismissive.

"Poker?" Charles repeated incredulously.

Donelli nodded. "Yes. It might be interesting, if we played for the right stakes."

Charles's breath whistled between his teeth, and Francesca stepped in front of him.

"Leave us alone," she said in a low voice.

"It's too bad, *bellissima*," Donelli said softly. "If you had only come with me last night, we could have made the world stand still."

Heat flooded her skin. "I'd never have gone anywhere with you."

His lips drew back from his teeth. "No?" he said, laughing. He bent and kissed her on the mouth, hard and fast, and then he stepped back. "It's been a pleasure seeing you again, Spencer," he said, before turning and melting into the crowd.

Francesca swung back to Charles. "Don't go after him," she said, but she needn't have bothered. Her stepbrother was standing absolutely still, staring blindly after Donelli, his face distorted with hatred.

"Charles?" Her voice was a whisper. "Charles—who is that man?"

"He's a son of a bitch, that's who he is." Charles's voice cracked. "He tried to steal Spencer's from us, but he failed. I got the better of him."

"What did you do? Did you bring charges?" Her voice trembled. "You should have. A man like that..."

Charles took her hand and tucked it into the curve of his arm. "And what did *you* do, sister, dear?" he said coldly. "No, don't deny anything. The details can wait until later. Now, all you have to do is smile."

"I want to go back to the hotel, Charles."

He squeezed her hand, hard enough so that she almost cried out.

"Smile, I said. That's right. Now, walk beside me calmly..."

"Please. I just want to——"

"People are watching, Francesca. Smile, so it all looks like an amusing joke. Good. And now we're going to play roulette, just as if nothing were wrong. Do you understand?"

She didn't. But then, she didn't understand much of what had just happened, she thought as she sank down on a stool beside her stepbrother.

Charles had said Maximillian Donelli had tried to steal Spencer's and failed, that he had got the better of him.

But it was hard to imagine Donelli failing at anything. And—God forgive her for her disloyalty—it was even harder to picture Charles getting the better of the man.

For a moment, Francesca felt the heat of his kiss on her mouth, and she touched her hand lightly to her lips. Her skin prickled, and she looked up, straight into Maximillian Donelli's eyes. He was standing on the other side of the gaming table, watching her with an intimate smile on his hard, handsome face.

Francesca's breath caught in her throat. Clearly, the evening wasn't over yet.

CHAPTER THREE

"MESDAMES et messieurs, faites vos jeux."

It was the croupier's call that set her free. Francesca gave herself a little shake and dragged her eyes from Maximillian Donelli's. She realized that Charles was talking to her, his tone slightly impatient, but she had no idea what he was saying.

"... know how?"

"I'm sorry, Charles." She swallowed. "I didn't hear what you said. Do I know how to do what?"

"Rien ne va plus."

"I was asking if you remembered how to bet the wheel, but it doesn't matter now. You've missed your chance."

"I don't much care. Can't we just leave?"

A muscle twitched in his cheek. "No, we cannot. I told you, people are watching. How will it look if that bastard gets the best of us?"

"What does it matter? Besides, how can he get the best of us if everybody knows he's a thief?"

Her stepbrother grimaced. "For God's sake, will you stop being so dense? The man's far too slick for anybody to know anything he doesn't want them to know. You don't see a sign on his forehead, do you?"

"But you said——"

"Dix-sept!" The croupier's voice rang out as the roulette wheel came to a stop. *"Noir, impair, et manque."*

"Seventeen," Charles muttered, "black, odd, and low." He gave a sharp bark of laughter. "Which means I lose on all counts."

"Charles——"

"Get that tone out of your voice, Francesca," he said sharply. "I told you, we're staying."

"Faites vos jeux, s'il vous plaît."

Charles leaned forward and plonked down several stacks of chips. The croupier spun the wheel and tossed the little ball, and he watched intently as it clattered along its path. There were murmurs from the crowd, even a soft groan as it came to rest on red thirty-two.

"Trente-deux. Rouge, Noir, pair, et passe."

Charles gave a little laugh as his chips were raked away. "Not doing very well, am I?"

"All the more reason to leave," Francesca said quietly.

"We leave after Donelli, not a second sooner." His voice roughened. "And the bastard's still here."

He hadn't needed to tell her that. She could feel those dark eyes on her; Donelli's steady gaze made her skin feel feverish.

"And now he's playing." Her stepbrother's voice sounded tight as a drum. "Good. It will be a pleasure to watch him lose."

But Donelli didn't lose, not then, not later. Like some illustrative mathematics equation, Charles's stack of chips seemed to diminish in direct proportion to the growth of the other man's. Maximillian Donelli seemed unaware; his lazy gaze drifted from the wheel to Francesca, never once coming to rest on her stepbrother. But Charles had begun to glare at him across the table. Spots of color rose in his cheeks each time Donelli won.

Francesca knew that you played against the house in roulette, but this particular game seemed to be changing into a private duel between the two men.

Her stomach knotted. Maximillian Donelli was up to something, but what? She had no doubt but that his every action had a purpose; he was the sort of man who went after a thing he wanted with single-minded determination. She had only to remember those moments in the garden last night to know that much. The way he'd taken her in his arms and kissed her, despite her protests, molding her body to his until he'd forced a response from her...

He looked up and his eyes met hers. A slow, insolent smile curved across his mouth, almost as if he'd read her mind.

She looked away quickly, but not before a telltale swath of pink blazed across her face.

"Charles—please, can't we——?"

The little ball clacked as the wheel spun again.

"Vingt. Noir, pair, et manque."

Charles cursed under his breath as the croupier raked in his chips. Across the table, Maximillian Donelli smiled as he gazed at his winnings. He made Francesca a mocking little bow, and she swung away and put her hand on her stepbrother's arm.

"This is ridiculous," she said sharply. "Haven't you had enough yet?"

His muscles knotted under her fingers. "Yes," he said, "you're right."

She puffed out her breath. "Good. I can hardly wait to——"

"It's time we had a go at something else. *Chemin de fer*, I think." He rolled his shoulders, smiled, and glanced quickly across the table. Her breath caught as she saw his smile slip, revealing the hatred that blazed just beneath it, but his mask was quickly back in place. "Come on, darling," he said, loudly enough for others to hear, "I can feel my luck changing."

But it didn't change. He lost with the first turn of the cards, and when Francesca heard the indrawn hiss of his breath she wasn't really surprised to look up and see Maximillian Donelli strolling to the table. He gave her that same mocking bow, then placed his bets.

And he won. Consistently—just as consistently as Charles lost.

When her stepbrother's last chips had been swept away, he put his hands on the table and stared across it. A silence fell across the room, as if everyone in it were caught in a warped pocket of time. Charles and Maximillian Donelli exchanged long looks. Charles's face was twisted with visible hatred, but it was the expression on Donelli's that frightened Francesca more.

He was smiling. Dear God, he was——

"Come."

Charles's hand clamped around her wrist. She trotted along beside him, praying that this meant he was finally giving up.

"Are we leaving?"

"Leaving?" He made a sound that she assumed was a laugh. "Don't be ridiculous. We're getting more chips."

"Charles, this is foolish——"

"And we're moving to the faro table." He smiled through his teeth as he slid an impressive stack of bank notes to the cashier. "I never lose at faro."

But he did lose, just as she had known he would, just as she knew she would look up and find her stepbrother's dark nemesis lounging against the opposite side of the table. Within moments, the pattern began again. Charles lost—and Maximillian Donelli won.

Francesca bit down on her bottom lip. Damn the man! Did he never lose at anything? And what was the point of all this, anyway? He was humiliating Charles—that much was certain. Their ugly little war was no longer private. There were eyes on them now, and whispers of amusement drifted in the air along with the cigarette smoke.

Whatever was going on had to stop.

She waited until her stepbrother was hurrying her toward the cashier again, then stepped quickly in front of him.

"Charles," she said quietly, "this is insane."

His lips drew back from his teeth. "I don't know what you mean."

"Yes, you do. You've lost a lot of money. And——"

"I can afford it."

"That's not the point."

"Don't tell me you're going to start moralizing." He laughed. "This is the wrong place for it, darling. This is Monte Carlo, remember? What are we here for, if not to gamble?"

"I'm not talking about gambling. I'm talking about—about this sick game you and that man are playing."

His eyes went flat. "I don't know what you mean."

"Yes, you do. You keep losing—and Maximillian Donelli keeps winning."

Charles's teeth ground together. "Yes. But he'll lose, sooner or later. It's just a matter of time."

"Charles, please. It's senseless . . ."

"Better listen to the lady, Spencer."

She spun around at the sound of that lazy, low-pitched voice.

"Mr. Donelli," she said furiously, "you have the damnedest way of turning up where you're least wanted."

His brows drew together in mock indignation. "Is that the thanks I get for trying to be helpful?"

"I didn't ask for your help."

Charles stepped in front of her. "Get the hell away from us," he said in a grating whisper.

Maximillian Donelli smiled, his teeth very white against his tanned skin. "The offer I made earlier still goes," he said pleasantly. "Just you and me, Spencer, *mano a mano.*" He looked at Francesca. "Have I got that right, sweetheart?" His voice was like silk. "I don't speak very much Spanish—perhaps you could check with the Marqués."

"Damn you." Francesca's voice quavered with suppressed fury. "What is it you want from us?"

All at once, he wasn't smiling any more. "Only what I'm entitled to," he said coldly.

"If that's supposed to be fraught with meaning . . ."

"Your stepbrother knows what I'm talking about."

Charles drew a rasping breath. "I told you," he said to Francesca, "he can't accept that we've taken away his best clients. That's the reason for this—this Old West shoot-out with cards instead of guns.''

Donelli rocked back on his heels. ''What's the matter, Spencer? Are you afraid to take me on in public, where your hands have to stay in sight all the time?''

Her stepbrother forced a smile to his face. ''You're drawing a crowd, Donelli. I thought you hated being in the spotlight.''

''I do. But I hate crooks even more.''

His tone was almost conversational, but it was loud enough to draw a titter from an onlooker.

Charles tried to laugh. ''What you don't like,'' he said, raising his voice a little, ''is losing.''

Maximillian Donelli smiled. ''Ah, but you're the one who's doing the losing tonight, Spencer. At faro, at chemin de fer, at roulette——''

''What's your point?''

He shrugged his shoulders. ''I told you. Take me on. Let's see which of us wins when the game isn't fixed.''

Charles licked his lips nervously. ''Everybody knows these are games of luck, not skill. There's no point in——''

''You're right. Roulette, chemin de fer, trente-et-quarante—they're all luck.''

''Exactly.'' Francesca could hear the barely disguised relief in Charles's voice. ''So we might as well——''

''Which is why I much prefer poker.''

Francesca's head came up sharply. There was a silken undertone in Donelli's voice now; looking at him, she thought of a cat patiently gauging the distance between its claws and the tail of a hapless mouse.

Be careful, Charles, she thought. You're walking into a trap.

''Poker's a game for riverboat gamblers,'' her stepbrother said dismissively.

Maximillian Donelli's lips drew back from his teeth. ''If you mean it requires enough skill and guts to put it out of your reach, I'd have to agree.''

Someone laughed softly. Charles's face paled, and he took a step forward.

"All right." His voice was low, the words almost guttural. "I've had enough. Name your stakes."

"No." Francesca spoke quickly. "Charles, don't. Please. He's been baiting you all along, don't you see? He's just been waiting to draw you in——"

"Did you hear me?" he said, shaking off her hand. "Poker, with a one hundred dollar ante."

Donelli smiled. "Five hundred," he said softly. "No limit."

"Charles, for God's sake..."

Francesca fell silent. Her stepbrother was already striding away from her, with Maximillian Donelli at his heels. After a few seconds, she drew a deep breath and followed them.

She had gone to a bullfight once, in Madrid. Charles had talked endlessly about the magnificence of the spectacle, the courage of the matador and the bravery of the bull, and the crowd in the stands had roared its agreement.

But all Francesca had seen was the desperation of a trapped animal; all she had smelled was the blood scent that hung in the warm air. After only a few moments of the first corrida, she had risen from her seat and fled. The elegant footwork of the matador, so appreciated by the crowd, had sickened her. It was all an awful game, she'd thought, watching as he'd taunted the bull with his scarlet cape. The poor, dumb beast kept attacking the swirling cape, while all the time it was the matador that would eventually destroy him and end their terrifying pas de deux.

Now, standing at her stepbrother's elbow in a quiet corner of a *salle privée*, she felt as she had felt then. Charles was intent on his cards; there was a grimness to his features, a determination that drew murmured compliments from the crowd. It seemed to be paying off, too. Her stepbrother had won the last three hands in a row. Compared to his, Maximillian Donelli's playing seemed casual almost to the point of contempt.

And yet—and yet, she thought, suppressing a tremor, she knew without question that the man with the dark as midnight eyes and that slightly contemptuous smile was going to emerge the victor.

She hadn't always thought so. When the game had begun, first one man had raked in the pot and then the other and she'd even let herself think Charles might just have a chance. Thinking it, she'd permitted herself a swift glance at Maximillian Donelli.

You're going to lose, she'd thought—and, as if he'd read her mind, that dark, proud head had lifted and Donelli's eyes had fixed on hers.

Her mouth had gone dry, and the intuitive knowledge of what was happening had twisted in her belly like a sudden, painful illness.

Charles had only been winning because Donelli had let him. He was playing with Charles, waiting for just the right moment to take him. And there was nothing she could do to stop it.

Francesca swallowed dryly as the image of the bull, brought to its knees, flashed into her mind again.

Stop it, she told herself, just stop it! It's only a card game, that's all it is. Charles will lose a lot of money, perhaps even humiliate himself, and then it will be over.

"Well?" Her stepbrother's voice was brusque. "Are you in or out?"

Donelli shrugged lazily, shoulders straining at the seams of his elegantly tailored dinner jacket.

"What the hell," he said, shoving a stack of chips toward the center of the table, "I'm in. And I'll raise you five hundred."

Her stepbrother shot a barely concealed look of triumph across the table. "I'll see your five—and raise you a thousand."

Donelli's lids came down like the shutter on the camera lens. "Here's your thousand," he said softly. "And I'll raise you three."

"Three thousand?" Charles's voice cracked, and Donelli looked up. He smiled carelessly, but his dark eyes were as hard as glass.

"No limits, remember? Those were the rules."

Charles's mouth tightened. "No problem, Donelli. Here's your three—and five thousand more." He smiled as much for the onlookers as for his opponent. "How's that grab you?"

Donelli nodded. "That's fine." He shoved a stack of chips across the table. "Tell you what, Spencer." He looked up, not at Charles but at Francesca. "How about another ten, just to make it interesting?"

She thought, for one hopeful moment, that Charles would toss in his cards. But the crowd's whispered delight was enough to urge him on.

"Ten it is," he said. "And fifteen thousand more."

The words were hardly out of his mouth before Donelli answered.

"Your fifteen," he snapped, "and twenty-five more."

Suddenly, Francesca thought of the heat of the arena and the matador's red cape goading the bull on. She wanted to shut her eyes and turn away, but to do that would mean defeat. Donelli might be able to humble Charles, but he'd never intimidate her.

There was a moment of silence and then her stepbrother slapped his hands against the table and pushed back his chair.

"I'm out of chips." Was she the only one who could hear the strain in his voice? Francesca wondered. "You'll have to wait while I buy some more."

"No problem." Donelli got to his feet and stretched lazily. "I can use the break."

Charles clasped Francesca's arm and hurried her out of the room. "Give me your money," he hissed.

She stared at him. "I don't have any money."

His hand tightened on her. "What do you mean? Of course you do. You must have something in that purse."

"Just a few small coins for the ladies' room." Then she remembered. "I do have some chips. The Marqués——"

"Give them to me."

"Charles——"

"Dammit to hell, Francesca! Just give me the chips, will you please?"

She dumped the chips into his cupped hands. He counted quickly, then uttered a harsh oath.

"What am I supposed to do with this? That bastard wants another twenty-five thousand."

"Then quit. Now, before things get worse."

Charles laughed coldly. "I can't quit," he said, as if even an idiot would understand that much. "Don't you see? The cards are with me. Donelli thinks he can bluff me out of the game."

"Charles." She drew in her breath. "You're going to lose. I can feel it in my bones."

He brushed past her. "I can't lose. My hand is good enough to beat anything he has. I'll write a check," he said tightly. "This time, I'm going to squash him for good."

But the manager politely refused. Surely Monsieur understood that there was a limit to how much credit the Casino could extend?

Charles's face was pale when he returned to the table, and all at once Francesca thought she could see the *espada* deftly concealed beneath the matador's elegant cape.

Was this it, then? Yes, she thought, of course it was. Charles would have to withdraw from the game, forced out by a lack of funds. It was meaningless, considering the enormous amount he'd lost tonight, but to a man like Charles, to whom appearance mattered more than anything, it was a humiliation he would long remember.

She stared at his opponent, hating him for what he'd done. Look up, she thought, look at me so you can see that I understand what you've done, so you can see that I hate you for it...

His dark head lifted slowly and his eyes met hers. Francesca's heart skipped a beat. No. There was more to this than she'd imagined. Donelli wanted more than humiliation. He wanted subjugation.

He stirred lazily, leaned forward, and smiled across the table. "I'll extend credit to you, Spencer," he said in a silken whisper.

Her stepbrother didn't hesitate. "Good." He spoke brusquely. "I'll write you an IOU."

"No IOUs."

"Very well. My personal check, then."

"Sorry." Donelli's teeth flashed in a quick grin. "No checks, either."

Her stepbrother flushed. "What the hell is this, Donelli? You said you'd extend me credit."

The other man straightened and folded his arms across his chest. All the sly amusement had fled his face, leaving it cold and empty.

"What I meant was that I'd be willing to let you wager something other than money."

"Other than..." Charles flushed. "I might have expected something like that from a man of your background. Okay, what will it be?" His lips compressed as he pushed back the sleeve of his dinner jacket. "My Cartier watch?"

Donelli smiled coldly. "Why would I want yours, when I have one of my own?"

"What, then?" Charles frowned impatiently. "My cuff links and studs? They're eighteen carat——"

Donelli sighed and tilted back his chair. "Cuff links. Good God, man, what do you think this is? A flea market?"

Charles's face purpled. "Listen," he said, "if you think I'm going to put up Spencer's——" Maximillian

Donelli laughed, and Charles's face grew even darker. "What *do* you want, then?"

A hush fell over the little gathering. In that last minute, before Donelli pushed back his chair and rose slowly to his feet, Francesca felt a sharp premonition of disaster. She took an unconscious step back, just as those dark, fierce eyes turned toward her, swept over her with insolent ease, then fastened on her face.

"What I want," he said, almost gently, "is your stepsister."

There was a second or two of stunned silence, followed by a peal of delighted laughter. Voices buzzed with excitement. Francesca heard it all, but none of it was as loud as the drumming beat of her own heart.

She stared across the table, telling herself that she'd misunderstood, but that hope slipped away as soon as she saw Donelli's face. The insolent smile was gone, replaced by a hard-mouthed determination that matched the forward thrust of his jaw.

Charles pushed back his chair, too. "What did you say?" he demanded.

Donelli's mouth softened. He smiled lazily, rocked back on his heels, and shoved his hands into his trouser pockets.

"You asked what I'd accept in lieu of your money, Spencer, and I told you."

"Charles." Francesca's voice was reedy, and she cleared her throat. "Charles, for God's sake, don't even dignify that with an answer."

"Never mind." Donelli's smile was the smile of a shark. "I knew you didn't have the guts."

Charles slammed his hand down on the table. "Done!"

Francesca stared at her stepbrother in disbelief. "Damn you, Charles, are you insane? You can't——"

"Let's see you beat this," he said, his voice slicing across hers with smug self-assurance as he fanned out his cards. A smile twisted across his mouth. "They're all diamonds." Donelli didn't move, and Charles began to chuckle. "You see?" he said to Francesca as he began reaching for the tumbled chips in the table's center, "There was nothing to worry about. A flush beats anything but——"

"This."

Everyone in the room seemed to hold their breath as Max Donelli turned over his cards, his movements unhurried and assured.

"One deuce," he said softly. "Two deuces." Francesca clasped the table's edge, her knuckles white as bone. Donelli lay down the remaining cards and smiled. "And three lovely ladies."

There was a collective gasp from the crowd. "A full house," someone said in awe. "Hell, who'd have dreamed it?"

No one would have, Francesca knew that. But this wasn't a dream, it was a nightmare. Did this—this barbarian really think he could win a woman in a card game, carry her off and—and...?

She glared as he rose and came slowly around the table.

"You're insane," she whispered.

His gaze swept over her again, lingering on the swift rise and fall of her breasts before returning to her face.

"Am I, *bellissima*?"

Heat spiraled through her veins. His words had been soft, a whisper meant for her alone, and they brought with them a swirl of memories: the scent of the flowers blooming in the garden when he'd kissed her; the feel of his arms as they'd drawn her to him; the warmth of his mouth...

She swayed dizzily, and Charles stepped to her side and put his arm around her shoulders.

"All right." His voice was hoarse. "What is it you really want, Donelli?"

"I told you. I want your stepsister."

Francesca twisted away from Charles's arm. "You bastard!"

Donelli smiled. "Perhaps we should continue this conversation in private."

He reached toward her and she pulled back like a hissing cat. "Don't touch me, you——"

"Francesca." Charles grasped her arm. "People are watching."

"Do you really care? You're the one who——"

"For God's sake, shut up!" His arm tightened around her; he made some light, inane remark that drew appreciative laughter as he marched her out of the *salle privée* and into a corner of the entry foyer. Once they'd reached it, he spun toward the dark-haired man who'd followed after them. "Okay," he said tightly, "what do you really want to end this farce?"

"You know the answer to that, Spencer."

Charles fumbled in his breast pocket. "I'll write you a check for twice the amount I lost."

"You can make it out for a hundred times the amount. I still won't take it."

"Damn you, man! What is it you want, then?"

"I want you to show some honor and stand behind your word." Donelli's voice was soft and dangerous. "Or is that impossible?"

"Listen, here, Donelli, maybe that kind of talk goes over big where you come from, but——"

"Stop it, both of you!" Francesca pushed free of her stepbrother's encircling arm, her eyes glittering wildly in her pale face. "How dare you treat me this way?"

"The man's an animal, darling, he——"

"And you're no better." She drew a shuddering breath. "Wagering me," she said, trembling, "as if—as if I were a piece of property."

"Francesca, darling——"

"This is not some—some desert kingdom. And I am not a—a slave girl to do your bidding."

"You would do mine, Francesca," Maximillian Donelli said softly, "if I asked."

Color flooded her cheeks as she swung toward him. "Never," she said grimly. "I'd never do anything you——"

His sudden smile disarmed her. "Dinner," he said, "and then dancing at the Sporting Club. A nightcap at the Living Room, and you'll be back at your hotel, safe and sound, by dawn. You'd do that, to redeem your stepbrother's debt, wouldn't you?"

Francesca's mouth fell open. "Dinner?" she repeated foolishly. "And dancing?"

"Unless you'd rather do something else. We can drive to Nice, or to Cannes——"

"You mean—you mean you want to take me out? On a date?"

He laughed and inclined his head. "I suppose that's the word to use, yes." One dark brow rose expressively. "Don't tell me you thought I had something else in mind?"

She stared at him while the color rose in her face again. What a bastard he was, she thought helplessly. He had made a fool of Charles and of her, and he had done it in front of the very people Charles worked so hard to impress. No one that had been witness to her stepbrother's humiliation would be likely to forget it; in fact, twenty-four hours from now, the story would have taken on a life of its own, embroidered so fancifully that neither she or Charles would ever be able to live it down.

She lifted her chin in cold defiance. "My stepbrother was right," she said carefully, "you're nothing but an ill-bred bastard. It's too much to hope that you'll ever pay for what you've done to us tonight, but I'll pray for it, nonetheless." She put a trembling hand on Charles's arm. "Come on," she said, "let's go to our——"

She cried out as Donelli's hand clamped around her wrist.

"Where the hell do you think you're going?" he growled.

"Let go of me, Mr. Donelli."

"I asked you a question. Where do you think you're going?"

"As far from the sight of you as I can get. You won. The game is over——"

"It won't be over until the evening ends. Weren't you listening, Francesca? Dinner, then dancing, then——"

Her eyes flew to his face. "You—you're serious, aren't you?"

"Absolutely." His smile turned chill. "That was the wager, and I've every intention of collecting."

She stared at him, then at her stepbrother. "Charles," she said imploringly, "please..."

His eyes slid from hers. "Just do it, Francesca." His voice was low-pitched. "Do it and get it over with."

"But—but I can't..."

Maximillian laughed as he slipped his arm lightly around her waist. "This will be an evening to remember, Francesca, I promise you that."

He started toward the door, and the pressure of his hand against her hip made it impossible for her not to go with him. She threw one last, despairing glance over her shoulder.

"Charles!" she called.

But her stepbrother had already turned away and begun striding back toward the gaming rooms.

She blinked as Donelli ushered her out of the door and into the perfumed warmth of the night.

"You—you can't do this," she said.

He didn't even bother answering, and why should he? she thought crazily as he led her toward a low-slung black sports car.

Maximillian Donelli made his own rules.

Francesca's heart banged against her ribs. He could do anything he wanted.

And, for tonight, she was his.

CHAPTER FOUR

DONELLI'S driving had a dangerous edge to it, the same as everything else she'd seen him do. The Ferrari leaped to life at his touch, the engine purring as a woman would if he stroked her, Francesca thought wildly, as she had done last night.

The thought drove her back in her seat so that her already rigid posture was ramrod straight. God, how she despised Maximillian Donelli! The man had somehow managed to make a fool of her twice in less than twenty-four hours. Her hands knotted in her lap. He had to know it, too—not that it mattered a damn to him. He hadn't said a word to her nor even glanced in her direction since they'd roared away from the Casino.

Well, that was fine with her. It gave her time to think about how she would get through the hours that lay like unmarked reefs in the dark channel ahead. They would be tricky to navigate, but she knew she could manage if she was careful. The first step was adjusting to what had happened to her, assuming that she could, somehow, adjust to being carried off by a pirate.

For that was what this man was, and never mind the expensive car or the custom-tailored dinner jacket. Max Donelli was a marauder who saw what he wanted and went after it.

And what he wanted tonight was her.

Her pulse rocketed. No, she reminded herself quickly, no, that wasn't true. Whatever he was, Donelli wasn't the kind who would force a woman into his bed. He wouldn't have to. He probably had difficulty keeping them out.

She cast a quick glance at him, her eyes sweeping over the straight nose, sensual mouth and proud jaw. He was

a hard-looking, handsome man, even she had to admit
that, but it was more than his looks that made him so
attractive. There was a toughness to him, a sense of
danger, that was as sexy as it was frightening. Even she
had responded to it, last night in the garden. He had
taken her in his arms and kissed her and——

"What are you thinking?"

"Nothing," she said, staring straight ahead.

He laughed softly. "There was such a soft look to
your mouth, Francesca—I hoped you might be thinking
of me."

Oh, God! Was it dark enough so he couldn't see the
rush of color his teasing words brought to her cheeks?

"You flatter yourself," she said in a voice that was
cool and steady.

The car swayed as it rounded a curve in the narrow
road. "Perhaps you were thinking of the Marqués."
Donelli glanced over at her. "I suppose I've disrupted
your plans for the evening."

"I hate to disappoint you," she said, even more coldly,
"but Charles and I planned to spend the evening alone."

The leather seat whispered softly as he shifted his
weight. "Such filial devotion," he said, his tone lending
mockery to the words. "It's charming to see in this day
and age."

Francesca's mouth narrowed. "I wouldn't have agreed
to this—this insanity if I didn't love my stepbrother."

"I've already said I find your—relationship
charming."

There was something in the way he said the word that
made her swing toward him.

"What is that supposed to mean?" she demanded.

Donelli shrugged lazily. "You and he are so close,
Francesca. He goes nowhere without you on his arm."
He smiled. "Not that I blame him. You're a very beautiful woman—what man wouldn't show you off, if you
belonged to him?"

"I don't 'belong' to anyone," she said sharply. "As for attending business functions with Charles——"

"Is that why you came with him to Monaco? Because the conference is a business function?"

"Of course," she said, hearing and hating the defensive tone in her own voice. "I've as much interest as my stepbrother in seeing that Spencer's does well."

"You and he share controlling interest in the company, don't you?" He glanced at her. "And you rubber stamp everything he proposes."

"I vote as Charles votes," she said sharply, "because he knows what's best for the business."

He smiled. "No wonder you're pleased with the job he's done. He's made lots of money for you lately."

Francesca puffed out her breath. "That's what this is all about, isn't it? Spencer's is doing well because Charles took clients away from you."

He laughed softly. "Yes. He certainly did."

"And you tried to take Spencer's from us." She waited, but he said nothing. "Good grief," she said with heavy sarcasm, "don't tell me you admit it?"

He gave another eloquent shrug. "Why should I deny what you already know? It's clear that your stepbrother keeps you well informed."

"He doesn't have to," she said coolly. "I told you, I trust Charles to make the proper decisions."

"You might want to rethink that," he said wryly, "in view of the way he's behaved tonight."

Color flooded her cheeks. "Which reminds me—just how far is Villefranche?"

"Don't you mean, will we be there soon?"

"That's exactly what I mean."

The Ferrari hummed as he changed gears. "Another few minutes." She felt him glance across at her. "The breeze has caught your hair, *cara*. Shall I close the windows?"

The words were simple, but he spoke them in a way that put an intimate twist to them.

"It's not necessary. And I wish you'd stop calling me that."

His brows rose. *"Cara?"*

"Yes," she said through her teeth. "I hate it."

Donelli smiled. "It's simply a term of endearment, Francesca."

"It's a meaningless affectation, Mr. Donelli. You're as American as I am."

"Am I?" he said, after a few seconds' pause.

"You're from New York, aren't you?"

"That's true."

"And I'll bet you were born in the States."

He looked at her. "New York Hospital," he said with a little smile, "just off East River Drive."

Francesca gave a decisive nod. "Exactly. Sprinkling Italian words into your conversation may win you lots of points with some women, but I'm not impressed."

There was another brief silence, and then he gave a soft laugh. "No," he said, almost thoughtfully. "I'm sure you're not. It would take more than a few foreign words to convince you that I'm not like all the other men you know."

But you're not. Her heartbeat stuttered. The words came into her mind so clearly and quickly that she thought, at first, she had said them aloud. She swung sharply toward Maximillian Donelli, but he was looking straight ahead, his eyes on the road.

Francesca drew a calming breath. "Exactly."

He smiled, as if she had said something amusing. "I'll see what I can do."

"Thank you," she said primly.

"You're welcome."

There was a hint of laughter in his voice but she ignored it. He could laugh at her all he liked, she thought grimly. What mattered was that she had won a very small, very tenuous victory. It was her first of the evening, and she had no wish to push her luck. The hours ahead were going to be difficult enough without antagonizing Maximillian Donelli any more than she already had.

Silence fell between them as the Ferrari raced through the night. Under other circumstances, she would have enjoyed the drive along the Corniche, the road that traversed the steep mountains that bordered the sea. There were three, each cut higher than the last into the craggy slopes. They were interconnected by narrow local roads that Donelli was using to move from one level to another. She had read that was the way to get the best views. Even in the dark of night, what she could see was spectacular. The lights of quiet villages flickered on the hillsides; other lights, brighter and more steady, crept slowly across the infinite blackness that was the sea.

"Have you driven the Corniche before?"

Francesca swiveled toward him. How did he do that? she thought irritably. His habit of seeming to know what she was thinking was disconcerting.

"No," she said.

"No, of course not. There hasn't been time. The shops by day, the Marqués by night..."

She drew a deep breath. "If you're trying to insult me——"

"I was simply commenting on the long hours you must have put in since you arrived on the Riviera."

"If you are, you're wasting your breath. There's nothing a man like you could say that would mean anything to me."

His soft laughter set her teeth on edge. "Is that your subtle way of warning me that we're not going to have a pleasant evening together?"

"I'm not trying for subtlety, Mr. Donelli. What's the point, when we both know that I'm here under duress?"

"Perhaps you'll have changed your mind by the time we drive back to Monaco." He glanced over at her. "There's a lookout point outside Villefranche where we can watch the sun rise." The car swayed as they rounded a curve. "You'll be able to see——"

"Thank you," she said coldly, "but I intend to breakfast in my rooms. Alone."

His leg brushed hers as he rearranged his long frame in the bucket seat. She tensed, then scooted farther into the corner. Donelli grinned.

"It's a little cramped in here, isn't it? I suppose you'd have preferred it if I'd hired a Rolls."

What she'd prefer, she thought furiously, was to have him turn the car around and take her back to her hotel. Her mouth opened, then clamped shut. No. There was no point in telling him that. He was certainly aware of it already. He was good at finding weaknesses in people. It was his speciality. He had known just how to get at Charles—— And at you, a little voice whispered. Aren't you leaving out what happened last night? He surely hasn't forgotten that, Francesca.

The thought made her sit up straight. Damn you, Charles, she thought furiously, this is all your fault! Her stepbrother had been a fool, and now here she was, trapped into paying for his foolishness.

Still, no matter what Charles had done, it was nothing compared to the machinations of Maximillian Donelli. What an unmitigated bastard he was! He'd probably planned all this from the minute she'd rebuffed him last evening.

No. No, he couldn't have. A frown creased her forehead. He hadn't even known who she was until they'd come face-to-face in the casino. Well, then, he'd managed this nasty little melodrama on the spot so he could get even with her and Charles both. Two birds with one stone, she thought bitterly.

Francesca gritted her teeth. Donelli wasn't a bastard, she thought grimly; the word didn't come close to defining what he was. Pirate. Thief. Marauder...

There was the soft sound of masculine laughter. "A penny for your thoughts, *cara*."

"I asked you not to call me that," she snapped.

"Take my advice, *carissima*," he said, the word a deliberate insult, "and make the best of the situation."

A flush rose in her cheeks. There *was* no best to this, she wanted to tell him, but even that would be more than he deserved. He had taunted her into more conversation than he had any right to expect; from now on, she was going to be absolutely silent. All he was going to get from her were "no's," and they would start as soon as they reached Villefranche.

No, she didn't want a drink. No, she was not hungry. No, she didn't want to dance—dance, for God's sake, *dance*—that was what he'd said they'd do, as if she were with him because she wanted to be, as if she'd ever, in a million years, willingly go into his arms...

"Have you taken a vow of silence?"

He was doing it again, she thought angrily, he was reading her mind. Francesca folded her arms across her breasts and held herself tighter. I won't answer you, she thought, I won't, I won't. She felt him looking at her, felt his gaze drift lazily over her body, his eyes lingering on the drift of crimson and pink fabric that clung to her like a second skin.

"You should have tried one of the others first." His voice was silken. "But then I can't imagine a woman like you managing poverty or chastity either."

The breath whooshed from her lungs. What was the point in keeping quiet if it meant letting this man walk all over her? Francesca turned to him, her eyes like cold stars in her pale face.

"A man who'll put up a fortune on a turn of the cards is hardly one to talk about poverty." Her voice was like ice. "And I very much doubt that you've ever been chaste, Mr. Donelli."

He looked at her, his teeth flashing in a quick smile.

"Max," he said.

"What?"

"I said, I'd prefer you to call me Max."

She stared at him in disbelief. "You must be joking."

He laughed softly. "A man and woman who are going to see in the sunrise together shouldn't be bound by the rules of formality."

"We are not a man and a woman," she said through her teeth. "We are two people going through some crazy charade to satisfy your monstrous ego. And I've already told you, we are not going to see the sunrise together."

"Ah, but we will. You know the terms of the wager, Francesca. Dinner, dancing——"

"The wager was that I'd suffer your company for the evening, and I am. As for what I call you, Mr. Donelli, I think you should be grateful I've chosen something that's acceptable in public."

The sound of her rapid breathing filled the air. She sat very still, waiting for his response. When it came, it was nothing that she might have expected.

Max Donelli smiled, and the look of it was dark and dangerous.

"Well, well, well," he said softly. "The kitten has claws."

"That's right. Sharp ones. And she's not afraid to use them."

"So I see." Suddenly, all the amusement fled his voice. "It's too bad your stepbrother doesn't have a little of your courage."

Francesca flushed. "It's no sin that Charles can't play your games, Mr. Donelli. No one could, except the devil himself."

"It's Max, Francesca. I've already told you that."

There was a note of warning in his voice. It registered in the rational part of her mind, but it did no good. Her anger had taken control.

"You can tell it to me until the cows come home. I am not——"

She gasped, lurching against the restraint of her seat belt as he braked and swung the wheel sharply. The tires squealed as the car jounced onto the narrow shoulder of the road. Donelli reached out, shut off the engine, and swung toward her, his broad shoulders and taut face blocking out the night.

"What do you think you're doing?" Francesca's voice shook.

"Your stepbrother and I made a bet." She pulled back as he reached for her, but there was nowhere to go. The door dug into her spine as his hands closed roughly around her shoulders. "You seem to have forgotten that."

"I haven't forgotten. How could I, when I'm here, trapped in this car with you?"

She caught her breath as his fingers imprinted themselves in her flesh.

"Trapped. Martyred. And you've no intention of letting me forget it."

She stared into his face, visible in the faint wash of moonlight reflected from the sea. Lord, he was angry! More than angry. Enraged. A tremor of fear tiptoed along her spine, like the feathery tread of some awful insect.

"I'm keeping my part of the deal," she said with deliberate calm. "We're on our way to Villefranche, for dinner."

"Dinner?" His laughter scratched across the silence. "What the hell is dinner, in the face of what your stepbrother owes me? It's meaningless, and you and I both know it."

"What do you mean, meaningless? That's what you said you wanted."

"I said a lot of things." His hands tightened on her. "But we were in Monaco then."

Francesca's heart turned over. "What are you saying?" She stared into his cold eyes. "You—you certainly don't—you can't expect——"

A smile as cold as the moonlight curved across his mouth.

"Can't I?"

"No." Her voice was reedy, so thin that she wondered if he could even hear it over the loud thud of her heart. "No," she said more strongly, "you can't. Not unless you plan on adding rape to your list of depredations."

His smile narrowed. "Ah, but it wouldn't be rape, would it, Francesca?" One hand slid to the nape of her neck and his fingers threaded into her hair. "All I'd have to do is take you in my arms, as I did last night."

"Don't," she said, twisting against him. "Damn you——"

"Do you remember how it was when we kissed?" He leaned toward her until she felt the warmth of his breath on her face. "Your mouth turned to fire under mine, your body to quicksilver."

Her hands came up and slammed against his chest. "I hate you," she said fiercely, "do you know that?"

Donelli laughed softly. "What has that to do with desire?"

"Charles was right. You—you're an uncouth barbarian, with the morality of a snake."

His fingers knotted in her hair, forcing her head back. "Don't ever confuse morality with manners, *cara*," he said roughly. "It's possible to exhibit the one without having any sense of the other. That is your stepbrother's error—he chooses to think that any kind of evil is permissible as long as he cloaks it in civilized dress."

"And you?" She forced herself to meet his eyes. "Is that what you think, too?"

His mouth twisted. "Are you really interested in the opinion of a barbarian?"

"You're the one who's talking about morality, Mr. Donelli." Francesca drew a shuddering breath. "You talk of seduction, but what I hear you describing is rape. If that's what you're planning, I find it difficult to see the difference between you and the kind of man you claim my stepbrother is."

For a moment she thought she had pushed him too far. His face darkened, his fingers tightened their grip on her until she almost cried out—and then, when she least expected it, he let her go.

A muscle knotted in his cheek. He whispered something in Italian, twisted away from her, and stared blindly through the windshield.

"If that's what you think of me," he said, lacing his fingers over the steering wheel so tightly that she could see the whiteness of his knuckles, "then I apologize."

Apologize? Max Donelli apologize? After everything that had happened, everything that he'd done, the very idea of his offering an apology was so ludicrous that she had to fight the rise of hysterical laughter in her throat.

"That's—it's all right," she said. It was, she knew, an inane remark. But he was waiting for her to say something, and she was still too stunned to think.

His fist slammed against the steering wheel. "It is not all right. I lost control of myself." He swung toward her, his eyes glittering. "That's not something I do often."

No, she thought, watching the proud, imperious face, she didn't think it was. And yet—and yet, he had lost control twice, once in the garden and again tonight, and each time she had been the cause.

The realization sent a sudden bolt of heat racing through her blood, as swift and electric as summer lightning. I did that to him, she thought, and she turned her face away from those dark, piercing eyes. He had almost seemed to read her thoughts before; God help her if he read them now, when she didn't even understand them herself.

"Francesca?"

She swallowed. "I—I accept your apology, Mr. Donelli."

"Max," he said. She looked at him, bewildered, and he smiled. "Surely my name isn't so difficult to say?"

It was little enough to give, now that the battle was over. Francesca smiled and inclined her head.

"Max," she said.

He puffed out his breath. "*Bene*. That's good." He leaned forward and switched on the engine. "And now——"

"And now you can take me back to my hotel."

He looked at her, smiling as if she'd made a poor joke. "But why would I do that?"

"Well, you just said—I mean, you apologized. I thought..."

She fell silent as he jammed his foot on the accelerator and swung the Ferrari onto the roadway.

"You thought wrong," he said pleasantly. "The night is young. We've dinner and dancing to look forward to, remember?"

"But—but..."

"Francesca." He took his eyes from the road just long enough to look at her and smile. "We'll have a pleasant evening, then I'll take you back to your hotel. Surely you can survive that."

She stared at him. "No. I mean, I could, I suppose. But——"

"There's Villefranche." She looked through the window and saw the lights of the town glinting just ahead. "I thought we'd have drinks in a little café just up the next road." She said nothing. His foot eased on the gas until the car was barely coasting, then he turned toward her, his face, illuminated by the eerie glow of the lights on the dashboard, a mélange of shadow and bone. "But if you prefer," he said, "we'll turn around and head back to Monaco."

"Yes. I mean, I think—I think..."

She stared at him. Why was she hesitating? He had offered her a way out and that was precisely what she wanted.

Wasn't it?

"Very well then, we'll go back. And don't worry about your stepbrother," he said, his voice purring in the darkness. "I'll explain that you tried to honor his debt but couldn't force yourself to do it."

Francesca closed her eyes wearily. Charles! She'd almost forgotten—but how could she? Charles's debt was the reason she was here. What would happen if she asked Max Donelli to drive her to her hotel? Would he consider her stepbrother's debt cancelled—or would Charles still be obligated to him? And, if he were, what would be the price Donelli asked in payment?

All she had to do was ask those questions of the man beside her. But how could she without making herself feel even more like a supplicant than she already did?

"Francesca?"

She looked at him from under her lashes. He was watching her and smiling, his expression unreadable. She slicked her tongue across her dry lips. She felt as if she'd been watching a chess game and had somehow missed the implication of some innocent maneuver. He had tricked her again, she thought bitterly.

"It's your decision." His voice was soft. "Shall we go on to Villefranche, or shall we go back?"

She hesitated. Just do it, Charles had said, do it and get it over with.

Francesca drew in her breath. "Villefranche," she said, and with that one word changed the course of her life.

CHAPTER FIVE

THERE was no scarcity of cafés along the Riviera. The world-famous towns that were strung along the coastline like gems in a glittering necklace were filled with chic night spots where the wealthy of two continents gathered to toast each other's good taste. They ran the gamut from self-consciously smoky little *boîtes* to sophisticated mirrored palaces. What they shared in common was that décor, while elegant, was never permitted to outshine the clientele.

Francesca had seen enough of such places to last her a lifetime. Cafés where people watching was the entertainment and the sole reason for existence flourished everywhere. Charles was addicted to them.

"Everyone who's anyone will be here," he'd said as he escorted her to a table at the Café de la Paix in Paris, and he'd shouted the same words over the shriek of the latest music at Annabel's in London.

And he was right. All the same faces gathered at all the same places. It was what they all wanted—Francesca understood that. You could kiss cheeks and talk up deals from one country to the next without ever losing a moment.

Now, as she stepped from the Ferrari, she glanced at the building ahead with little interest. It was small, white-stuccoed with a red tile roof that seemed to cling desperately to the steeply sloped hillside. A week ago she'd have believed it old. But she knew better now: Charles had taken her to such a place just the other evening.

"You're going to love it," he'd assured her—and she had, at first glance, until she'd realized that the tile roof was false and the dark ceiling beams molded plastic imitations.

"I think you'll find this place different," Max Donelli said as he took her elbow and led her in the door.

Francesca didn't bother answering. What was the point? She would not find it different, but that didn't matter. Her likes and dislikes were of no importance tonight. This was his show, from start to finish. She was just along for the ride.

Still, the room they entered caught her by surprise. It was long and narrow and filled with the blue haze tossed off by heaven only knew how many lit Gauloises. The room hummed with sound, not from a discreetly hidden compact disc player or a deliberately displayed neon-lit juke box, but from the conversations and laughter of its patrons, not a one of whom would ever be found on the society pages of a newspaper or magazine.

Francesca paused uncertainly and glanced up at Max. "Are we in the right place?" she asked softly.

He laughed. "What's the matter, *cara*? Isn't this up to your usual style?"

She stared at him. Was he the sort who liked to go slumming? She wouldn't have thought it, somehow, but then what did she know about the man except that he'd cheated Charles in some kind of business deal? Her mouth narrowed. He was from the gutter, Charles had said. Well then, anything was possible. She knew some people had a taste for this kind of thing: she'd been with Charles's crowd in Paris when they'd dragged her off to a bar in Montmartre where they were the only people dressed in evening clothes.

"Isn't it a scream to see how the other half lives?" a girl had kept saying, but Francesca had only found it embarrassing.

She pulled free of Max's hand. "If this is your idea of a joke..."

He sighed. "Go straight on through," he murmured. His fingers clasped her elbow again and he moved her forward. "That's right. Head for that doorway."

His hand was firm, and she had no choice but to do as he asked. She moved ahead of him stiffly, aware of the eyes that moved over her silk-clad figure, and she turned on her heel as soon as they stepped through the door that led into the adjoining room.

"I agreed to a drink," she whispered fiercely, "not to lording it over the locals. So if that's your idea of a good time——"

"Is that what you think?" Her stony silence was his answer. Max's mouth narrowed. "I see that you're still judging me by your stepbrother's standards." His hands clasped her shoulders. "Turn around, Francesca."

"What for?"

"Because I tell you to," he said tightly, and he spun her away from him.

The breath caught in her throat. They had not entered another room, they had stepped into the night sky. That was how it seemed, at first: the stars hung just beyond her reach, lighted by an ivory moon, and the black Mediterranean glistened far below.

"Oh," she whispered.

Max laughed throatily. "Yes," he said softly, "oh!"

She swayed backward, caught by a sudden dizzying vertigo, and his fingers cradled her shoulder.

"Easy," he said, drawing her back against him. His body was hard against her back, his breath warm against her cheek as he bent his head to hers. She could hear the smile in his voice. "Are you all right?"

She nodded. "Yes. I just—I didn't expect..."

"Nobody does. I suppose I should have warned you about Stefan's terrace."

Francesca gave a little laugh. "Is that what it is? I thought, for a minute, I'd stepped out into space."

Slowly, as her eyes adjusted to the darkness, it all came into focus. They were standing on a terrace that seemed to have been carved out of the face of the hill. Candles flickered on small wooden tables scattered about the stone floor, with only a wrought-iron railing to separate the terrace from the night. The sound of the sea beating against the rocks below was a counterpoint to the silence. The rising moon was climbing from a black sea into a blacker sky, stretching like a ribbon of cream from the terrace into the darkness.

"Shall we sit down?"

Max's voice was soft; his breath ruffled the curling strands of hair at her temple. A tremor raced through her, and she swallowed and stepped away from him.

"Fine."

He led her to a table and she slipped into a chair. "Well? What do you think? Do you like this place?"

She looked across the table at him. It's wonderful, she thought, I've never seen anything like it. But she wasn't about to admit that to him. She had already shown too much of herself to this man. For the rest of the night, she would not like or dislike anything. She would simply endure.

"It's very nice," she said politely.

Max grinned and leaned toward her. "If that's the best you can manage, don't tell Stefan. You'll break his heart."

"Stefan? Who is——?"

"*Ah, Max, c'est toi! Bienvenue. Ça fait a cinq—non, six mois que nous ne t'avons pas vu. Comment vas-tu?*"

"*Stefan. Je vais très bien, merci; et toi, mon ami? Ça va bien?*"

Francesca looked up as Max scraped back his chair and got to his feet. The man called Stefan was obviously the café's proprietor. She watched, bemused, as the two greeted each other with back-slapping embraces. Max switched to English long enough to introduce her. Stefan smiled and bent over her hand, and then the men slipped back into a French that was far too swift and colloquial for her to follow. But she had no trouble understanding the last of their conversation, when Max ordered champagne and Stefan laughed and chided him gently.

"After all this time," he said in French, "do you think you need to tell me what it is you drink when you have a beautiful woman on your arm?"

Max looked at her, then said something so softly that she couldn't hear it. Her cheeks flushed as Stefan smiled. Whatever the joke was, it had been at her expense.

"Stefan is an old friend," Max said, when they were alone again. "We've known each other for——"

"What did you say about me?"

His brows rose. "What makes you think I said anything?"

"I don't speak much French, Mr. Donelli——"

"Are we back to that again?"

Francesca blew out her breath. "The point is, I understood just enough of what you and he were saying to——"

"You understood just enough to take offense, Francesca, but with no reason. You're right, we did talk about you. Stefan said you were beautiful, and I corrected him." He smiled at the look that came over her face. "I see that bothers you, *cara*."

"It doesn't," she said stiffly. "I don't care what you——"

"I told him," he said softly, "that you were much more than beautiful. I said that you were the loveliest woman I'd ever seen."

His words sent a whisper of pleasure along her spine.

"It is the truth," he said as their eyes met.

There it was again, that faint hint of an accent. She had heard it several times now and she'd come to recognize it as a sign that he was under some kind of stress.

Or coming on to a woman. Her mouth turned down. Yes. That barest suggestion of an accent, as phony, she was certain, as his dramatic name and the way he peppered his conversation with "*cara*'s and "*bellissima*'s probably knocked 'em dead. Well, it didn't mean a thing to her. If Max Donelli really thought he could turn the clock back to what had happened last night in the garden,

if he for a second hoped he could charm her into forgetting the reason she was here in the first place——

"Did you hear what I said, Francesca?"

She shrugged, her shoulders moving lightly above the
softly draped bodice of her silk gown.

"I heard you," she said carelessly.

His smile dimmed a little. "But such a compliment
means nothing to a woman who has heard them all many
times before."

Her eyes met his. "Don't feel badly," she said sweetly.
"I'm sure it's a line that's worked wonders on all the
other women you've paraded through here."

Max leaned back in his chair and grinned. "Ah, *cara*,
forgive me. You wanted me to tell you that you were the
first."

"I asked you not to call me that. And I don't care if
I'm the first or the fiftieth——"

"But you *are* the first."

He fell silent as their waiter brought the Dom Pérignon
he'd ordered. Max waved away the obligatory first
tasting. He waited until their glasses had been filled and
tiny bowls of grilled sardines and crudités were placed
before them, and then he leaned across the table toward
her and grinned.

"The first woman I've ever won in a card game,
anyway."

Francesca flushed. "I'm afraid I don't find that terribly amusing," she said stiffly.

He sighed. "No. I suppose not." He watched her for
a moment, then lifted his glass and held it out toward
her. "What shall we drink to?"

"I don't care to drink at all, thank you very much."

"Don't you like champagne?"

"It isn't that."

"We can have wine, if you prefer, or an aperitif."

She drew in her breath. "I don't want anything to
drink, Mr. Donelli."

"Max. We've already settled that, remember?" There was a sudden hard edge to his voice. "Perhaps we should go over all the ground rules for tonight. If you wish to discharge your stepbrother's debt——"

"If?" She laughed incredulously. "Believe me, I wouldn't be here otherwise."

"No?" His smile was quick and sly. "I gave you a choice in the car, Francesca. I offered to take you back to Monaco. You chose to come with me instead."

Her chin lifted. "Because I chose to cancel Charles's debt."

His lips drew back from his teeth. "Exactly. Which means you agreed to drink with me, dine with me——"

"That doesn't mean I have to like it."

"That remark hardly becomes you, *cara*." His tone was harsh. The seconds ticked away while they looked at each other, and then he smiled lazily. "Anyway, you should be flattered."

"Flattered? To be here with you?" She smiled grimly. "I was right about that ego of yours. It's probably big enough to fill a football stadium."

"I was referring to the way in which you came to be with me tonight."

Francesca stared at him. "Being won in a card game is hardly flattering. And I've asked you and asked you to stop the *'cara'* and *'bellissima'* business. If you think that impresses me——"

"Is that what I'm trying to do?"

The note of amusement in his voice made her blush but it was too late to retreat.

"Maybe."

Max crossed his arms over his chest. "And how did you arrive at that conclusion?"

Her color deepened. "Now you're trying to embarrass me."

"It's a simple question, Francesca. Can't you manage an answer?"

There was a few seconds' silence. "Because of what happened last night," she said finally. "If you think I've forgotten——"

"No." His tone softened and his gaze slipped over her. "I didn't think you had."

"What I mean is that you're wasting your time, if you think—if you hope that I'll find all this a—a turn-on."

His expression was bland. "You think I've set all this up to seduce you? The game of poker, the bet with your stepbrother—— "

"This charming little café, the champagne." Her chin rose. "It's occurred to me," she said. "Yes."

"And?" His voice was like silk. He leaned closer and his hand curved around her wrist, his fingers stroking lightly across her skin. "Let's assume, for the moment, that I had gone to all this trouble on your account." His smile grew catlike. "Would all my efforts have been wasted?"

She pulled her hand from his, but not soon enough. He laughed softly, and she knew he had felt the sudden leap of her pulse under his fingertips.

"No," he said, answering his own question, "no, I think not."

"You can think what you like. There's no sense in arguing with that ego of yours." Francesca tossed her head. "I just want to be certain we understand each other. I've had champagne before. I've been called pet names before——"

"Yes, I'm sure you have."

His tone set her teeth on edge. "Does that disappoint you, Max?" She gave him a honeyed smile. "Were you hoping I'd gone through life untouched, just waiting for you to come along?"

A muscle danced high in his cheek. "What if I said yes?" He bent over the table and the flame of the candle turned his eyes into diamonds. "What would you say then, *cara*?"

Her heartbeat stumbled as she looked at him. She knew what he thought of her—he'd made that clear enough—and it didn't matter a damn. He was nothing to her; after tonight, she would never see him again.

Still, she couldn't help wondering what he would say if she told him the truth, if she met his cold gaze unflinchingly and said that she had never been intimate with a man, that she had never even responded to one as she had to him last night? Her eyes slipped to his mouth and suddenly she remembered the feel of it against hers, remembered the heat of his kisses and of his body...

"Francesca?"

His voice was soft, like liquid flame. He reached out and touched her cheek, his hand light against her skin.

His fingertips were a breath away from her mouth. She had only to turn her head and she could touch her tongue to his flesh, taste him...

Stop it, she told herself, stop it, stop it!

Francesca drew away and reached for her wineglass. "I'd say," she said, after a long swallow of champagne, "that you were a little old to still believe in fairy tales."

Max's mouth thinned. "A woman who doesn't flinch from the truth, hmm? Your stepbrother could take lessons from you, *cara*."

"There you go again. I keep telling you——"

"A slip of the tongue," he said, holding up his hands in mock surrender. "It's just that certain words and phrases come easiest to me."

"Of course they do," she said coolly. "French, with Stefan. English, with Charles. And with your women you develop that tiny little accent and drop little bits of—what is it supposed to be? Italian?"

His brows rose. "Yes. Italian."

"Mmm." She took another swallow of wine. Her throat felt parched, and it was foolish to let the wine go to waste. "Italian. To go with your name. Where'd you pick it from? A playbill?"

Max began to laugh. "The name—and the language—came from my father. I'm sorry if it displeases you."

"It doesn't displease me. It doesn't mean anything to me, one way or the other. You can call yourself what you like. I told you, I'm not impressed."

"But you should be flattered."

"So you said. But——"

"You accused me of setting all of this up, Francesca. Well, I didn't—much as I'd like to claim I did." He laughed, although the sound of it was chill. "But then, no one has to lift a finger to help Charles Spencer make a fool of himself. He has a knack for managing that all on his own."

"That's not true. I was there, remember? You lured him into that card game."

Max shrugged his shoulders dismissively. "I only plead guilty to making the most of an opportunity." His teeth flashed in a quick smile. "Two opportunities, in fact."

"Two?"

"Yes. The first was taking Charles in." His eyes swept over her face while a slow smile curved across his mouth. "The second was having the good sense to name you as the night's prize."

Waves of color rose beneath her skin. "I don't like the way you say that. You make it sound as if—as if..."

"I expect only the pleasure of your company, Francesca."

She took a sip of wine. "Just so long as you remember that."

Max smiled lazily. "How could I forget, *cara*? I suppose I'll simply have to make the most of the little you're willing to offer me, won't I?"

He was still teasing her. She could hear it in his voice, see it in his eyes. Her breath caught. She had the power to change that mocking tone. All she had to do was look across the table at him and say—and say...

"What are you thinking, Francesca?"

Her eyes flew to his. He spoke softly, with almost careless indifference, yet she had the sudden awful feeling he was reading her thoughts again. She tore her gaze from his. God, her head was buzzing. What was the matter with her?

"Nothing," she said, clasping her hands in her lap, "nothing at all."

"Are you sure?" The corners of his mouth lifted in a quick smile. "You looked so pale."

She swallowed dryly. "Did I? Perhaps—perhaps I'm hungry. I haven't eaten in hours."

Stupid. Stupid! How had that slipped out? It was true, but she hadn't planned on eating. She gave a mental shrug as she lifted her glass and drained it. What did breaking bread with him prove? Nothing. Absolutely nothing.

"Where are we going for dinner?" she asked with a polite smile.

Max lifted the bottle of Dom Pérignon and refilled her glass. "I hadn't given it much thought." His eyes flickered from her glass to her lips as she raised it again. "How about La Coupole?"

"Without reservations? You can't——" She broke off when she saw him smile. "Forgive me," she said coolly, "I forgot. I'm sure you can get a table anywhere you like."

"La Coupole is too noisy. The Grill at the Hôtel de Paris, perhaps?" A frown creased his forehead. "No. I'm sure you've had dinner there already."

"I have. Twice." She put down her glass and looked directly at him. "Which reminds me, Mr. Donelli——"

This time, his smile was almost gentle. "Max."

"Max. Where do *you* dine? For that matter, where do you stay? Everyone who's attending the conference is at either the Hôtel de Paris or the Hérmitage, but I haven't seen you at either."

His brows rose. "Have you looked for me?"

"No," she said, making a face, "of course I haven't. But I'd have noticed you, if——"

She caught her lip between her teeth as he began to smile.

"Go on," he said softly.

Francesca blew out her breath. "It's just that—that one keeps bumping into the same people, in the elevators and corridors..." Her eyes swept to his, and she blushed and looked away. "Never mind," she said, lifting her glass. "It doesn't matter."

Max watched her in silence and then he pushed back his chair and got to his feet.

"Will you excuse me for a moment? I have to make one quick phone call." His smile was dazzling. "And then I'll show you where I've been staying. Would you like that?"

"I told you, it doesn't——"

"And I'll take you to dinner at my secret place. How does that sound?"

Francesca smiled. "Secret? A secret restaurant here, on the Riviera? What does that mean, that it's only got one star in the Michelin?"

Max laughed, too. "I'll just be a minute. Why don't you finish your champagne while I'm gone?"

She watched him make his way into the café, and then she stared at her wineglass. It was full again—when had that happened? A warning rang in her head as she reached for it, but she shrugged it aside. She wasn't the one who was driving, she thought with a little laugh. Max was. And it would damned well serve him right if she fell asleep in the car while he drove.

That might not be what he'd meant by wanting the pleasure of her company, but it would be more than he deserved.

Her head was buzzing dangerously by the time they reached the car. "Are you all right?" Max asked solicitously as he helped her inside.

"Fine," she answered.

But she wasn't fine. The car seemed to be moving even before he turned on the engine. She closed her eyes as he swung on to the road, but that was a mistake. Closing her eyes only made her feel dizzy. Had she drunk too much champagne? No, she'd only had a glass. Two, maybe. Or three...

"Do you like lobster, *cara*?"

She stirred in her seat. "Lobster?" she asked muzzily.

Max nodded. "Lobster. And mussels. I trust you like both."

Francesca cleared her throat. "Could you open the windows? It's a bit warm in here."

The night air made her feel a little better. She sat up straighter and put her hand to her forehead.

"Does your head hurt?"

She glanced at him. "How do you do that?" she asked irritably.

"Do what?"

"You seem to know what I'm thinking even before I've finished thinking it."

He grinned as he shifted gears. "Magic, *cara*."

"And don't call me that," she said wearily, leaning back against the headrest.

He laughed softly. "Sorry."

"You're not sorry at all."

"But I am. I've no wish to anger you, Francesca."

She sighed and closed her eyes. "That's not true."

"Are you calling me a liar?" His tone was teasing.

She rolled her head to the side and opened her eyes. "Not a liar, exactly."

He smiled. "Then what, exactly?"

"You're—you're..." She sighed. "What you did to-night wasn't right. Luring Charles into that card game——"

"What did your stepbrother tell you about me?"

She turned her face away from him. "Enough to know that you tried to steal Spencer's."

"What would you say if I told you he was lying?"

"Charles wouldn't lie to me."

"Is that your answer?"

She looked directly at him, her jaw thrust forward. "Did you expect something different?"

There was a moment's silence, and then Max shook his head. "No." His voice was without expression. "No, I suppose not."

"Is that what this is all about? Did you think you could get me to change my stepbrother's mind about you?"

Max laughed. "It never crossed my mind."

"Good." Her voice was grim. "Because—because..." She sat up straighter and peered out of the window. "Where are we?"

"Nice." He swung the wheel and they turned down a narrow street that seemed to be leading to the water. "Haven't you been here before?"

"No. Charles promised, but..." She shrugged. "He's been busy."

"Yes, I'm sure he has." He pulled the car to the curb and switched off the engine. "Come, Francesca. Let me show you my favorite restaurant."

She waited until he came around to her side of the car and then she swung her legs out of the open door. Max took her hand as she got to her feet.

"I can manage on my own," she said, pulling away from him.

She could, but only with effort. Her legs felt a little rubbery, as if she'd been out climbing mountains all afternoon. Max made an impatient sound and put his arm around her waist.

"I told you, I can——"

"Of course you can," he said in a soothing whisper. His arm curved more closely around her. "But you're wearing high heels. You don't want to catch them in the cobblestones, do you?"

It was a reasonable precaution, one with which she couldn't argue. Besides, her legs really did feel strange—

as if they were filled with champagne instead of bone and muscle. She choked back a giggle.

"Something amuses you, *cara*?"

She almost told him that everything amused her all of a sudden: her wobbly legs, her muzzy head, the way Max's accent seemed to be gaining as they grew closer to the water.

The water. Francesca frowned. Why were they heading toward the sea?

"Is there a restaurant down here?"

"The best in the world."

"But where? I don't see——"

"Good evening, Luigi."

"Buona sera, Don Maximillian."

She blinked. A man had stepped out on the path before them. He was dressed in pressed jeans and a dark chambray shirt.

"Tutti sono pronto, signore."

Max nodded. *"Va bene."*

Francesca looked at him. "Do you know this man?"

He smiled. "Luigi works for me. Watch your step—the planking is slippery."

She glanced around her. They were walking along the dock, moving farther and farther from the street.

"I don't understand," she said slowly. "You said there was a restaurant..."

"Signorina."

Luigi was standing beside a sleek launch, his hand outstretched. Francesca looked from him to Max.

"What does he want?"

"He wants to help you board, *cara*."

"Board?" Francesca came to a dead stop. "What do you mean, he wants to help me board?"

Max sighed. "The boat, Francesca."

The idea chilled her. "No," she said, digging in her heels, "I don't want to."

"Francesca. Don't be silly. You said you wanted to see my secret restaurant and my hotel."

She stared at him, trying to read his face, but it revealed nothing.

"Max——"

His smile was cool. "Ah," he said softly, "the lady knows my name."

"Max, what's this all about?" She peered out to sea. "Is there a floating hotel out there? I never heard of one, but——"

"No." His arm tightened around her. "There's no floating hotel."

"Well, then, what——?"

"Get in the boat and I'll show you."

Francesca looked up at him. Her heart was beginning to pound, but that was crazy. Max Donelli was a hard man, a powerful one, but there was no reason to fear him.

"Why?" She gave what she hoped sounded like a laugh. "It's a nice boat, Max, but if you're going to try and convince me that it houses a hotel and a restaurant——"

"*Signore, per favore...*"

Max nodded. "*Si, Luigi, si.*"

She looked from one man to the other. "What's he saying?"

"He's reminding me that it's getting late. Our meal will be cold."

Francesca stared at him. "What in heaven's name are you talking about?" Her brows rose. "Is this boat yours?" When he said nothing, she looked at the launch again. It was sleek and handsome, and suddenly she pictured the cozy little table that had probably been set for two in the cabin below. "If you think I'm going to dine alone with you on that——"

He laughed. "Turn your head a little, *cara.*"

"What?"

"Your head." Max put his hand against her cheek and turned her gently toward the water. "What do you see?"

She frowned. "The Mediterranean, of course."

"What else?"

"What is this, Max? I'm not much for guessing games——"

"Tell me what else you see, Francesca."

"Lights," she said irritably. "For God's sake——"

"If you look closely," he said gently, "you can see that they're on a boat."

Francesca blinked her eyes. Yes, he was right, she could see a boat just beyond the marina. A big boat. Fifty feet. No, a hundred——

"One hundred and thirty-seven, to be precise," he said, still in that same surprisingly gentle voice.

She stared at him, too confused to wonder whether she'd spoken aloud or he'd read her thoughts again.

"Is it yours?"

He nodded. "Of course."

"You mean…" She blinked again. "You mean, that's where you're taking me for dinner?"

Max laughed softly. "There's nothing like the sea air to perk up an appetite, *cara*."

She looked across the dark water again. The boat—Max's boat—was only a few hundred yards away, but suddenly—suddenly, Francesca felt as if he were asking her to join him on another continent.

"No," she said. Her voice was breathy. "No," she said again. She took a step back. "I'd rather not. Thank you for the offer, but——"

She cried out as Max swung her up into his arms and stepped onto the deck of the launch.

"Andiamo, Luigi."

The seaman bent to the lines that held the launch to the dock, and the boat swung free.

"You can't do this," Francesca said, struggling in his arms, but he only laughed and held her tighter.

"Can't I, *cara*?" he said, and she watched, horrified, as the dock grew smaller behind them.

CHAPTER SIX

FRANCESCA was not a stranger to private yachts. In her stepbrother's high-powered financial world, such vessels were often seen as corporate perks. She had gone to her fair share of parties and weekend cruises aboard a dozen or more different corporate cruisers.

But she had never been on board anything the equal of this boat. Even now, when she was so taut with anger that it seemed difficult to breathe, she knew that this was surely the biggest, most elegant yacht she had ever seen.

It loomed over the launch as they drew aside. Luigi cut the engines just as Francesca twisted free of Max's unwelcome embrace. She stood trembling, arms wrapped around herself, hands massaging the skin he'd bruised, fighting against the fear that lay just beneath her rage.

Max made her a mocking bow. "Welcome to *Moondrift*."

Her brain worked feverishly for a cutting reply, but what could you say to a man who'd just carried you off? Max saw her consternation, she was sure of it, because he laughed softly as he extended his hand to her.

"Let me help you aboard."

She cast one last, hopeless look toward the shore, although she knew it was useless. The marina was deserted at this hour of the night. No one would be able to help her. Luigi hadn't even offered a sympathetic glance as she'd struggled wildly in his employer's arms.

"Francesca?"

She looked at Max Donelli, her gaze sweeping from his outstretched hand to the ladder dangling down the side of the ship. It looked, she thought with a shudder, a hundred feet high, but she knew she'd sooner brave the Matterhorn than accept his help.

"Don't touch me," she said coldly. She took a deep breath and stepped decisively onto the landing stage, grasped the railing, then began to climb, her thoughts less on the deep, dark water below than on the man behind her and the view he must have of her hips and legs as the wind swirled her skirt into a silken froth.

It seemed to take an eternity to get to the top, but eventually she reached the deck and found herself face-to-face with a pleasant-looking man wearing an officer's cap.

"Are you the captain?" she demanded.

He touched his hand to his cap and smiled. *"Bonsoir, mademoiselle."*

Francesca gave him a steady look. "I'm here under duress."

His smile never wavered. *Pardon?"*

"I said——"

"I'm afraid Captain Dussage speaks only French, *cara.*" Max smiled at her as he slipped his arm lightly around her shoulders, and then he lapsed into conversation with *Moondrift*'s captain.

It was all she could do to keep from bursting into hysterical laughter. A crewman who spoke only Italian and a captain who spoke only French. Well, why not? *Moondrift* might as well be flying the Jolly Roger. She was a pirate ship, her crew dredged from every seedy port in the world, with a—a lying Blackbeard ensconced in the owner's cabin.

She gave Dussage a cold look but it was wasted on him. His attention was focused on Donelli. What was Max telling him? Her French wasn't good enough for her to follow. She had a swift, foolish vision of Madame Monserat trying to hammer Conversational French into the unwilling heads of the girls at boarding school. If only she'd paid attention! Was Max giving orders to raise anchor and put out to sea? Her anger had kept her fear in check but now she felt it rise along her skin in clammy waves.

What would happen next? Anything was possible. Anything.

Dussage turned away, and Max began urging her forward. Francesca dug in her heels.

"You'll never get away with this," she said tightly. "Charles knows I'm with you, had you forgotten?"

Max chuckled. "Such dramatics, Francesca. Whatever are you thinking?"

"I'm not going with you, dammit! You'll have to—to——"

"You have a choice," he said softly. "You can either come quietly, or——"

She tossed back her hair as she faced him. "Or what?" Her chin rose in defiance. "What will you do, hmm? Have one of your henchmen shackle me and drag me to your cabin?"

The corners of his mouth lifted. He was laughing at her, damn him!

"What a fascinating idea, *cara*. I've never tried such games, but they sound interesting."

Francesca's cheeks blazed with color. "There are laws against this," she hissed. "I'll see to it you pay for what you've done."

He laughed as he drew her forward with him. His strength was far greater than hers; she had no choice but to hurry alongside, her heels tapping lightly on the polished teak deck.

"I already am. My men will laugh for weeks about the night I had to force a woman aboard."

"I suppose they usually come willingly," she said, twisting against his hand as he led her below. "I suppose——"

"They do, if they've heard of Jean-Paul."

"Jean-Paul?" Francesca grimaced as Max clasped her wrist in one hand and pushed open a door with his other.

"Who's he, the crewman in charge of the prisoners' cell rack...?"

Her voice faded as Max propelled her into an elegant, spacious dining room. She stared at the polished birchwood table set for two, the candles and flowers that were its centerpiece, the fine china and sterling at each setting. Overhead, a crystal chandelier blazed with light.

"Jean-Paul," Max said smoothly, "is the finest chef this side of the Pyrenees." Max shut the door behind them and leaned back against it, arms folded across his chest. "I see you're disappointed, *cara*." Sarcasm coated his words like honey. "Did you expect to find something else behind this door?"

Francesca flushed. "What is this?" she demanded.

Max's brows rose. "Perhaps it's more important to determine what it is not," he said as he strode to the bar that curved across the far wall. "You will notice, for example, that it is not my cabin." He touched a button and a mirrored wall panel slid open, revealing racks of Swedish crystal. "You'll notice, too," he said wryly, "that it isn't a wall-to-wall bed, covered in black satin sheets."

She swallowed. "All right. Maybe I did think that— that—— "

"What this is," he said, taking a bottle of Perrier-Jouet from a small fridge, "is Café Donelli." He stripped the foil from the neck of the champagne bottle, then eased out the cork so that it made a dull pop.

"But you said—you said you'd take me to your favorite restaurant..."

"And I have," he said gently. "I dine on board as often as possible." The champagne foamed as he poured it into a pair of crystal flutes. "I sleep on board, as well." He held out a glass to her and smiled. "So much for my evil intentions, *cara*."

Was it true? She flushed darkly. "That doesn't make up for anything. You took advantage of me. You—you fed me too much wine, and then——"

There was a knock at the door and a white-jacketed steward stepped into the room.

"Bonsoir, monsieur. Mademoiselle."

Max turned toward him and spoke. His French was swift and almost impossible to follow, but certain words came through with great clarity. *Homard. Pâté. Salade verte. Profiteroles au chocolat. Espresso...*

Francesca closed her eyes, then blinked them open. It was true. He was ordering dinner. That really was the reason he'd brought her here.

So what? The reason didn't matter. What counted was that she was here against her will. Max Donelli had simply carried her off, and nobody seemed to give a damn! The seaman, Luigi, had heard her cry out, he'd seen her struggle wildly in Max Donelli's arms, but he hadn't even offered her a sympathetic glance. Captain Dussage had shown no interest at all in the fact that Max had practically dragged her below. And now there was another crewman, standing not three feet from her, hanging on his employer's every word and she—she might as well be invisible.

Max turned to her as soon as the door closed after the steward. "I took the liberty of ordering dinner for the both of us. Some pâté, lobsters, green salad——"

"Are your crewmen all deaf?" Her mouth tightened. "Or are they simply blind?"

His brows rose. "If there's some deep meaning to that, *cara*——"

"I want to be taken ashore. At once."

"When Jean-Paul's already begun our meal?" He smiled and held out a glass of champagne. "You'd hurt his feelings."

"You've already filled me with enough wine, thank you very much."

"Another of my heinous crimes," he said pleasantly. "Tying women down and force-feeding them champagne."

"You took advantage of me. All that wine——"

"All the wine did was mellow you a bit." He smiled lazily. "Is that such a terrible thing?"

"As for Jean-Paul," she said, as if he hadn't interrupted her, "I don't give a damn about his feelings. I want to——"

"You're behaving like a spoiled child." His tone was suddenly harsh. "We don't always get what we want in this life, Francesca. You should have learned that by now."

"You're a fine one to talk. "You—you dragged me on to this damned boat——"

"And what would you have said if I'd simply asked you to come with me? Would you have agreed?"

She touched the tip of her tongue to her lips. "I—I don't know."

"The truth, *cara.*"

Francesca drew a breath. "All right," she said. "I suppose—I suppose I wouldn't have. But you can't blame me."

"No. I cannot." Max's voice was grim. "Your stepbrother has filled your head with poison about me."

"It isn't poison. Charles told me——"

"The point is, you would have refused." He turned away and touched the wall panel. Soft music welled up and filled the salon. "And so we'd have dined at the Cygnet or some place like it, where the story of how we came together has already been embroidered a thousand times over."

The story of how we came together. Francesca swallowed dryly. The way he said it lent a special meaning to what had happened. An intimacy, as if—as if...

"Which would have been ridiculous, considering that we'd already given Monaco enough to buzz about." He smiled as he took a bottle of Perrier from the refrigerator and uncapped it. "Why should I have taken you some place where we could have given them even more?"

Francesca watched as he filled a glass with ice and then poured the mineral water over it.

"That didn't seem to bother you at the Casino," she said slowly.

"Much to my regret." An embarrassed smile edged across Max's mouth as he handed her the glass. "I let myself be carried away, I'm afraid. Public displays aren't my style."

No, she thought, she didn't think they were. Charles had said Max Donelli didn't like the spotlight, but the light had surely been focused on him tonight. Now that his anger had run its course, he was probably regretting the rashness of his actions.

But if he hadn't been rash, if he hadn't played Charles for stakes that were so high, she wouldn't have been with him now...

Heat flooded her cheeks. She turned away quickly and put the cool glass of Perrier against her cheek.

"You're probably right," she said. "Walking into a restaurant together would be like taking center ring at the circus."

"Exactly." He came up behind her and put his hand lightly on her shoulder. "Now," he said quietly, "will you join me for dinner?"

Francesca turned slowly and looked at him. "I—I don't know. I..."

A muscle knotted in his jaw. "It's all right," he said. "I understand." She watched as he put down his glass and walked to the door. "I'll have Luigi ready the launch——"

"No." Her heart gave a funny little lurch, as if it had missed a beat and were racing to catch up. "No," she said when he turned toward her, "that's all right. It— it would be foolish to do that. I mean, we're here already, and dinner's almost ready..." Her voice trailed away. "I'll have dinner here."

Max's smile lit his face. "I'm glad," he said, only that, but the words sent a tremor dancing along her spine.

*   *   *

Dinner was not as good as Max had promised, it was better. The pâté had been velvety, the mussels sweet and bursting with flavor. Even the salads were extraordinary, laced through with walnut kernels and goats' cheese and tasting of a delicate vinaigrette.

By the time the lobster had been served, Francesca was laughing at Max's story about the first unhappy time he'd tasted mussels.

"They were like little rubber bullets, do you know what I mean? I chewed and chewed but they never got any smaller or softer, and there I was, seated at the place of honor beside my hostess..."

She laughed as she pushed aside her plate, propped her elbows on the table, and rested her chin in her hands. Charles wouldn't have approved, but then, he wouldn't have approved of the way she'd eaten her lobster, either, with her fingers as much as with her fork.

"It tastes better that way," Max had said, and he was right. The meat seemed sweeter when it was coaxed from the shell. Max...

Francesca blinked. When had that happened? When had she begun to think of him as "Max"? He'd asked her half a dozen times tonight to call him by his first name but she'd refused. Now, without even realizing it, she'd slipped into not only using it but thinking it, too.

She smiled to herself as she watched him pick up a lobster claw and crack it open. Somewhere between the moment the steward had served the lobsters and now, that was when it had happened. After all, how could you call someone Mr. Donelli when you and he were both eating with your hands?

"Good?"

She looked up. "Yes," she admitted, "it's delicious."

"I'm glad." He gave her a mischievous smile. "But you must leave room for dessert, or Jean-Paul will be disappointed."

He went on talking, telling her an involved, funny story about chocolate profiteroles, of all things, and, although she smiled and laughed in all the right places, she wasn't really paying attention. She was concentrating, instead, on the animation in his face and the expressive way he gestured with his hands, and she thought suddenly how easy it would be to like Max Donelli very, very much.

But it was too late to think that way. She had made a fool of herself with him last night, first going into his arms with an abandon that had shocked them both, then running from him like a frightened schoolgirl. What must he have thought? And what must he think of her now? A flush rose in her cheeks. She knew the answer to the question. What could he think about a woman he'd won in a card game, a woman offered up as a surety for a wager? Her hands began to tremble, and she wiped them on her napkin, then folded them carefully in her lap.

Max saw the change in her immediately. "*Cara*, what's the matter?"

She shook her head. "I just—I just realized that it's getting late. I think perhaps it's time you took me home."

"It's more than that, *cara*. A moment ago your face was alive, and now——"

Her heart gave a panicked stutter. "Don't," she whispered before she could stop herself.

"Forgive me. I know you don't like me to call you that——"

She shook her head and looked down at the table, her hair falling around her face like a pale cloud.

"I—I meant, don't—don't do what you were doing."

Max frowned. "I don't understand."

She took a deep breath as she raised her eyes to his. "You—you won the right to have me with you tonight. Surely you realize that was embarrassment enough."

"Is that why you think I made the wager with Charles? To humiliate you?" His voice roughened. "I had no such intention, Francesca. Your stepbrother and I were playing for high stakes——"

"You don't have to go through it," she said quickly. "I saw it all, remember?"

"But you misunderstood what you saw." Max pushed back his chair. "Charles agreed to stake something in lieu of cash."

"Please. I just asked you not to——"

"That meant he had to risk something very valuable." He paused, and she could hear the swift leap of her pulse. "And what could that possibly have been except you?"

His words whispered into the silence. Francesca stared at him while she searched for something to say, a clever rejoinder that would shine with sophistication, but her tongue felt as if it were stuck to the roof of her mouth. All she could do was look at him while his eyes, black as obsidian, moved over her face like a caress.

The air was suddenly too thick to breathe. Quickly, she pushed back her chair and got to her feet.

"Please—take me back to Monaco."

Max's mouth twisted. "You can't keep running from me, Francesca." He moved quickly, rising from his seat and coming around the table to her like a lithe jungle cat closing in on its prey. "My people have a saying—what fate puts before you cannot be escaped." He reached out his hand and cupped it around the back of her head. "This is fate, *cara*. Why are you afraid to admit it?" His fingers threaded into her hair.

"Please." Her throat was dry, her words as insubstantial as grains of sand on a sun-baked desert. She rose to her feet. "Please, Max, take me back."

"No." His voice was rough as raw silk. "Not yet."

"You said I could leave whenever I liked. Well, I—I——"

"Dance with me first, Francesca."

Her eyes widened. "What?"

"One dance," he said as he gathered her into his arms, "and then I'll do whatever you ask."

"Max——"

"I promise." He began moving in rhythm to the music that had been playing softly all through dinner, and slowly she began moving with him, her body stiff at first, then growing dangerously pliant in his arms.

A thousand warnings prickled along her skin, but how could she move away from him? He was holding her too closely and besides—oh, God. She didn't want to move away, she wanted to feel his arms tighten around her as they were now, to feel the beat of his heart quicken as hers was quickening...

His hand cupped her head and she sighed and let it rest against his shoulder. She felt the whisper of his breath on her cheek as he bent and brushed his mouth against her temple.

How could it feel so right to be in his arms? Max Donelli was a stranger. He was more than that—he was her stepbrother's enemy, he was *her* enemy, the man who had, only hours before, disgraced Charles and her both. Did he think she'd forgotten?

She tried to draw back but he wouldn't let her. His hand slid to the nape of her neck; he urged her head to his shoulder again. No, she thought, no—but her treacherous body had its own will. She felt as if she were clay made for the sculpting touch of Max's fingers.

He whispered her name as she closed her eyes and relaxed against him, and then he murmured something in Italian so softly that it seemed part of the music to which they danced. His hand slipped down her spine, moving gently over her gown, stroking her until she couldn't tell what was silk and what was flesh. She whimpered as his fingers traced the curve of her buttocks and he said her name again, slurring it on his tongue as if it had been immersed in honey.

"Cara," he said, *"bellissima mia."* Her eyes opened and met his, and she caught her breath at what she saw blazing in the night darkness. "I want you, Francesca." He bent to her and teased her lips apart with hot, hungry kisses. "Tell me you want me, too."

His mouth slanted across hers in a kiss as fierce as it was sweet. She felt her body clench tightly in response.

"Tell me, *cara*."

The words he wanted to hear danced into her head like shadows moving on a screen. They would have no substance until she said them aloud. But how could she? How...?

"Francesca." He cupped her face in his hands and tilted her head back, and then his mouth closed on hers over and over again in urgent, wet kisses that deepened with each silken glide of his tongue. His hands swept down her back and cupped her buttocks; she moaned his name as he brought her body tightly against the excited hardness of his.

"I love the way you say my name," he said thickly. "Say it again, *cara*, and then let me taste the sound of it on your lips."

All reason fled. She was trembling in his arms, burning with a heat that only his kisses could assuage. Her head fell back, her lashes fluttered to her cheeks.

The soft tap on the salon door exploded into the silence like a gunshot. Francesca spun out of Max's arms. He cursed softly and stalked to the door. She turned away as he wrenched it open and rattled off a string of Italian phrases, his tone harsh enough so that she didn't need to know the words to understand their meaning.

She caught a glimpse of the steward's pale face.

"Mi dispiace, Don Maximillian," he stuttered, holding out a piece of paper. *"Ma il capitano dice che era urgente."*

"Give it to me," Max growled, snatching the paper from the steward's hand.

She watched as he scanned it. He looked up and crumpled it in his hand.

"Va bene," he said, "it's all right, Giacomo, you did the right thing."

Francesca turned away as the door closed. It seemed like a long time before Max came up behind her and put his hands on her shoulders.

"Francesca?" he said softly.

She drew a shuddering breath. "Please." Her voice was a whisper. "Please Max—it's very late. Take me back to Monaco."

She looked down as he turned her slowly to him. "Look at me," he said, putting his hand under her chin and gently lifting her face to his. "Is that what you really want?"

His voice was soft with promise. No, she thought wildly, no, it wasn't. What she wanted—what she had almost done—was insane.

"Yes," she said, forcing her eyes to meet his, "it is."

"Why?" His voice was bitter. "Because of your stepbrother's lies?"

"Please, don't start that again. You've had what you wanted tonight..."

"The night's not over, *cara*."

Something in the way he looked at her frightened her. "It is," she said quickly. "It will be dawn soon, and you said——"

"I know what I said." He turned away and picked up the bottle of champagne and the crystal flutes. When he looked at her again, he was smiling pleasantly. "We'll start back soon, I promise. But first, tell me, have you ever seen the Mediterranean sky from the deck of a ship at night?" She shook her head, and he looped his arm lightly around her shoulders. "Let me show you what you've missed, *cara*."

Francesca hesitated. She wanted to go with him, which was a good reason for holding back, but that didn't make sense. Nothing made sense any more, not the way she'd fallen into his arms nor even the fact that the word *cara* no longer grated across her nerve endings.

"What is it?" He smiled. "Are you afraid the ship will turn into a pumpkin at midnight?"

She gave herself a mental shake. "How could I fear that when it's long after midnight already? And you did promise you'd have me at the hotel by sunrise."

There was the briefest pause before he answered. "We could be far from Nice by dawn, Francesca."

She looked up at him, caught by some undercurrent in his voice. But, before she could speak or even wonder about it, he pushed open the companionway door and led her out on deck. The sight that greeted her drove every thought aside.

It was that darkest moment that came just before dawn. The sky was a black velvet canopy shot through with silver, the sea an ebony plain undulating gently under a breeze that bore the spicy scents of Africa.

"How beautiful," she whispered.

Max filled the flutes and held one out to her. "I agree," he said, his eyes on her face.

She flushed. "No wine, thank you."

"A toast, Francesca."

She hesitated, then took the glass from him. The night was almost over and she'd come through it safely. That was something to drink to, wasn't it?

Max touched his glass to hers. "*Salud,*" he said softly.

She sighed as she sank into one of the chairs. "The sky really is lovely," she admitted.

He sat down beside her. "Have you ever counted the stars?"

Francesca smiled. "Actually, I tried once. My sixth-grade class went to the Planetarium. Have you ever been to one?"

He shook his head. "No, never. What's it like?"

"Oh, it's a fantastic place. They take you into this enormous domed room and the lights dim and you look up and you see a million billion stars."

"Like these?"

She drank some more wine. "No, they're not like these at all. These seem so close I feel I could almost... Look!" She pointed out toward the horizon. "Did you see? A falling star."

"Quickly, *cara*, you must close your eyes and make a wish."

She smiled. I wish, she thought, I wish—I wish this night might never end...

When she opened her eyes, Max was looking at her. "What did you wish for?" he asked softly.

Her heart lurched. "I wished—I wished——" She tore her eyes from his and thrust her empty glass toward him. "I wished for more champagne," she said brightly.

He hesitated, then smiled. "Of course. I'm glad you like it."

She felt the chill effervescence explode inside her mouth as she drained the champagne from the flute, then rush to her head in a swirl of bubbles.

"I don't think I'd better drink any more," she said with a little laugh, "not unless you're prepared to watch me sleep all the way back to Monaco..." Her words drifted away as she looked at him. He was watching her with a dark, strange expression on his face. "Max? What is it?"

"What if there had been no card game tonight? What if I had simply asked you to come away with me."

Francesca frowned. "I don't—I don't understand."

"Yes, you do." His voice was taut. "Would you have come with me?"

No, she started to say, of course not, but then she remembered what he'd said when he took her in his arms. "What fate puts before you cannot be escaped." How could she deny the truth, when the stars were all around them and the champagne and the taste of his kisses were on her lips?

She drew a deep breath. "I think—I think, perhaps, I might have," she whispered.

She waited, her heart pounding rapidly, wondering what she would do if he took her in his arms again. Minutes seemed to pass and then, to her surprise, he got to his feet. "It's getting late," he said in a voice curiously devoid of inflection. "Wait here until I get your wrap and bag from the salon."

"I'll come with——"

"No." He put his hands on her shoulders and pressed her back into the chair. "You sit here and finish your wine."

"No more wine." She gave a rueful little laugh. "I've had too much as it is."

"Then close your eyes and rest." His voice was gentle. "I'll just be a few minutes."

She lay her head back as his footsteps faded. The night was over, then. A bittersweet sorrow rose up within her and she thought suddenly what it would have been like if she had met Max Donelli some other way...

Francesca sighed and closed her eyes. It wouldn't have mattered. He was Charles's enemy; the way they met wouldn't have changed that, and Charles said he was a thief.

Her eyes closed. A thief. Was he? Or was he only a brigand? Not that there was much of a difference. Not that it really mattered...

Francesca's breathing deepened. Seconds later, she was asleep.

CHAPTER SEVEN

FRANCESCA came awake slowly, rising toward the beam of light that lay across her face, centering her growing consciousness on it in a desperate attempt to still the sharp tattoo of pain inside her skull.

She blinked her eyes open, then groaned softly and rolled onto her belly. She didn't remember opening the curtains last night, but she must have; her hotel room was filled with bright sunlight. Was it time to get up already? It couldn't be—she'd only gone to sleep a couple of hours ago. It had been almost dawn when—when . . .

When what? Memory came slowly: the Casino, the café in Villefranche, then dinner aboard *Moondrift* . . . Sudden images flashed into her mind. Soft music; Max, taking her in his arms, kissing her, touching her . . .

She sat up quickly. Too quickly. The room lurched; she felt its gentle motion in the pit of her stomach. Carefully, she shut her eyes and leaned her head back against the headboard. Think, she told herself, think. She'd gone on deck with Max, they'd had some wine and talked, although she couldn't remember what they'd talked about, and then—and then——

And then, nothing. She had no recollection at all of the trip back to Monaco nor even of entering her hotel room. How could that be? Surely she'd remember . . .

Her heart gave a funny little lurch as she lifted her lashes. Her gaze swept around the room again.

"Oh, God," she said, as if the whispered plea might change reality.

But it didn't. The simple fact was that she was in bed, but she was not in her hotel room. She was still on board *Moondrift*—and the yacht was under way. The faintly perceptible sense of motion was not in her belly, it was real.

Her heartbeat did its strange gallop again and she forced herself to take a deep breath. Easy, she told herself, easy, there was sure to be a perfectly rational explanation of why she was here instead of in her hotel room, why she was lying in a wide, satin-sheeted bed wearing—wearing nothing but her silk teddy.

Francesca groaned softly. Of course there was an explanation. All she had to do was think of it.

She fell back against the pillows. All right, she thought frantically, let's try it again from the beginning. Drinks at the little café, then the surprise of the launch ride across the water, then dinner... A flush rose beneath her skin and she pushed the all too vivid memories aside. They'd gone up on deck next, she thought with grim determination, and—and what?

Francesca pushed the covers aside and swung her legs to the floor. The sudden movement sent her head spinning, but that was better than sitting here trying to remember what had happened last night. How had she gotten from the deck to this cabin? She glanced down at herself, then clutched the sheet and tugged it to her throat. Maybe the better question was how had she ended up undressed and in this bed?

Her fevered brain raced through the litany again. Drinks. Dinner. Deck. The breath whistled from her lungs. Bits and pieces were drifting back. They'd gone on deck to see the stars. Max had poured champagne. They'd talked about this and that, she couldn't recall what exactly, it was all fuzzy...

What if I had simply asked you to come away with me? Would you have come?

She caught her lip between her teeth. Max's voice seemed to echo inside her head. Had he really asked her that? No. He wouldn't have; he knew by now that her answer wouldn't have been one he wanted to hear.

Would it?

Francesca closed her eyes. She'd had far too much to drink last night, that was the trouble. If she hadn't, she'd have awoken in her hotel room this morning instead of in this cabin. And she couldn't really blame Max for it, either. He'd left her on deck alone while he went below.

"I'll be right back," he'd said.

Something like that, anyway, and she'd settled in to wait—and she'd fallen asleep, instead.

She groaned and put her hands to her face, lightly massaging her temples. Be honest, Francesca. You passed out, you didn't fall asleep. And Max had found her that way; he'd probably decided the simplest thing was to let her sleep it off in one of *Moondrift*'s cabins, then deliver her safely back to Monaco in the morning. Francesca's hands fell to her lap. Wasn't that going to set tongues wagging? Max's yacht docking in the harbor and she stepping off it, still dressed in last night's finery.

She gave herself a little shake. There was no sense in lamenting what was, she thought as she wrapped the sheet around herself and got to her feet. The yacht would be docking soon—the trip from Nice to Monaco couldn't be a very long one—and she wanted to be ready to leave *Moondrift* the moment it did. Her brow furrowed as she looked around the cabin. Where was her dress, anyway? Not at the foot of the bed or draped across the chintz-covered chair near the windows. In the cupboard, then. Whoever had put her to bed must have...

Her breath caught. And just who had that been? she wondered. Who had stripped away her dress and tucked her beneath the satin sheets?

There was a light rap at the door. Francesca drew the sheet more closely around herself and turned toward it.

"Who is it?"

"Buon giorno, signorina."

It was a girl's voice, light and pleasant. Francesca's brows rose in surprise.

"Come in," she called.

The door swung open and a young woman wearing a black dress and white apron stepped into the cabin.

"*Signorina.*" She smiled pleasantly. "*Io porto il suo caffè,*" she said as she crossed the room and deposited a small serving tray on the night table.

Francesca nodded. "Thank you."

The girl smiled again. "*Non c'è de che, signorina. Che cosa posso fare per lei?*"

Francesca smiled and shook her head. "I'm sorry. I don't speak Italian."

"*Ah, si, io capisco. Maria.*" The girl pointed to herself. "*Io sono Maria, signorina.*"

"How far is it to Monaco, Maria?"

"*Mi scusi?*"

"Monaco. Will we be docking soon?"

"*Ah, Monaco. Si, si.*" Maria poured a cup of coffee and put it on the table. "*Monaco è là,*" she said with a flick of her head.

Francesca nodded. It was a relief to know that she'd figured it out right. She wondered if Max had notified Charles of the delay. She hoped he had, otherwise her stepbrother was bound to be worried about her.

"Do you know if anyone phoned my brother?"

Maria smiled blankly. "*Mi scusi, signorina. Non parlo inglese.*"

"You don't speak English? Well, then, is there anyone on board who does? Is there... *Est-ce que une personne* who—who does *parlez inglese?*"

The girl giggled at the bastardized combination of French and Italian, but at least she seemed to understand it.

"*Si. Don Maximillian parla inglese.*"

She added something else, a question, and it didn't take much effort to figure out what she'd asked.

"No," Francesca said quickly, "don't—don't bother the *signore*. I'll do without a translator until I'm dressed. Which reminds me—where are my things? My clothes?"

She reached out and touched the girl's dress, then pointed to herself. "Do you know where my dress is?"

Maria's face lit. She nodded happily and pushed open the closet door. *"Essi sono molti vestiti per la signorina."*

The closet was filled with women's clothing—dresses and skirts and floor-to-ceiling shelves of what looked to be sportswear. The only thing that seemed to be missing was Francesca's own evening dress. She sighed. What did it matter? She could borrow something—the leftovers of one of Max Donelli's lady friends, no doubt—and have it returned to him later.

"Grazie, Maria."

It took a while to convince the girl that she didn't want any help dressing, but finally Francesca was alone again. Two cups of the strong black coffee cleared her head along with some aspirin from the adjoining bathroom. By the time she took a pair of white cotton pants and a pale yellow T-shirt from the open closet, she felt almost human again. There was an assortment of canvas shoes and leather thong sandals on the bottom shelf. She slipped her feet into a pair, combed her hair, and then took a deep breath.

All she had to do was face Max one last time and that wouldn't be very difficult, not with the sun shining brightly overhead, and then she'd be back in Monaco, safe and sound at Charles's side.

Then why was she so nervous? Francesca paused at the door. Maria had referred to Max as Don Maximillian, just as Luigi had last night. It had seemed an affectation then, like the faint accent and Italian-sprinkled speech, but suddenly, despite the bright sunlight and familiar, cheery smell of freshly brewed coffee, the old-fashioned title had a realistic and surprisingly oppressive sound to it.

"You're just being silly," she said firmly. She ran her fingers through her hair, squared her shoulders, and marched out into the corridor.

The ship was very quiet. The sandals she'd chosen were a little large; they slapped softly as she made her way toward the companionway and she had to stifle the instinct to rise up on tiptoe. The cabin doors she passed were all shut, and she began to wonder if she might get off *Moondrift* without seeing Max at all. It was probably too much to hope for, but it was a possibility. It felt as if it was still early in the morning: maybe he was still asleep in his cabin. Yes, she thought as she stepped from the companionway, why not? There was no reason for the master of *Moondrift* to be awake yet; he could very well be...

"Good morning."

Her head came up sharply. Max was leaning back against the rail, smiling, and she had the uneasy thought that he'd been waiting for her. Her gaze swept over him. She had never seen him dressed this way, in snug, faded jeans and an equally faded gray T-shirt bearing a Columbia University logo. He hadn't shaved this morning—there was a dark shadow along his jaw—and the breeze had ruffled his dark hair so that it lay in disarray across his forehead. Don Maximillian, indeed, she thought.

"Did you sleep well?"

She swallowed dryly. "Fine, thank you. I—I'm sorry if I caused you any trouble last night..."

His smile tilted wryly. "You were no trouble at all. How's your head?"

"My head?" She gave him a quick, sharp look. "What do you mean?"

He shrugged lazily. "I was just wondering if the aspirin I gave you did the trick. I wanted you to take three tablets, but you insisted you'd never be able to keep down that many."

She stared at him blankly. "I don't remember any such conversation."

He laughed as he turned toward the sea and leaned his elbows on the railing. "I'm not surprised. You were pretty much out of things by then."

"Pretty much out of..." Her voice faded away. Was he teasing her, or had she really said—and done—things she couldn't recall? Color swept across her cheekbones as she thought of awakening in that sumptuous bed dressed in nothing but her teddy. Who had put her there? Worse still, how could she bring herself to ask him such a question?

"You were asleep when I carried you to your cabin." He looked at her. "But you awoke—for a little while, anyway—when I put you to bed." He grinned as the color in her cheeks intensified. "That was what you wanted to ask me, wasn't it?"

There he went, reading her thoughts again. Francesca gave him a cold look. "You really ought to consider taking that act on the road."

"What act?" he asked innocently.

"Why didn't you ask Maria to take care of me?" she demanded, ignoring his question.

"Maria?" His smile was intimate and amused. "The sun was kissing the mountains when I put you to bed, *cara*. Surely you didn't expect me to disturb Maria's rest for such a simple chore? A few hooks and buttons aren't difficult."

Damn the man! He was laughing at her. Well, if he expected to get a rise out of her, he was in for a disappointment.

"Nothing you haven't done before," she said sweetly.

Laughter glinted in his eyes. "Forgive me for disillusioning you. I keep forgetting how much you would like to be first."

She swung away from that dark, sardonic smile and stared past him to the sea. A little furrow appeared between her brows. She hadn't given it any thought, but, now that she looked, where was the coast? Nice was barely a stone's throw from Monaco. Surely you could see land as you traveled.

"What is it, Francesca?"

"Nothing, really," she said, forcing aside a vague sense of unease. "I just wondered—I assumed we'd sail much closer to shore."

Max took her arm. "Let's have breakfast, shall we? What would you like? Fresh fruit? Croissants? Or do you prefer an American breakfast—bacon and eggs, perhaps, or sausage?"

"More coffee is all I want, thanks." She glanced at him as he led to the aft deck where an umbrella table had been set up in a sheltered corner. "Anyway, is there really time for breakfast?"

"There's plenty of time," he said as he drew out her chair. "How do you take your coffee? Black? Or with cream and sugar?"

"Black is fine, thanks." She waited as he poured coffee for the both of them. Aside from the little taunts about having put her to bed, he was really being very civilized this morning and that surprised her. She'd half expected him to go on and on about last night and what had happened when they'd danced...

What if I had simply asked you to come away with me?

She blinked. Why did she keep remembering those words?

"You must try some of these berries. And some *crème fraîche* with them. Or would you prefer——?"

"Did you phone my stepbrother?"

"That's been taken care of."

Francesca nodded. "Good. He'd be awfully worried otherwise."

"Would he?"

"Of course." She looked at him. "You have the wrong idea about Charles—not that it's necessary for me to defend him."

A tight smile curved across his mouth. "I'm afraid that you couldn't do that if you tried."

She put down her cup and pushed back her chair. "There's no sense arguing about it," she said. "Anyway, it doesn't matter now. We'll be docking soon, and——"

"We've at least three hours before we dock. You might as well relax and eat something."

"What? What did you say?"

Max lifted the cover from a silver serving dish. "I said that you ought to eat something. Jean-Paul's made omelets——"

Her eyes fixed on his face. "Did you say something about not docking for three hours?"

He shrugged as he reached for the coffeepot. "Perhaps not. Captain Dussage says it may take a little longer. Shall I refill your cup?"

Francesca felt the abrupt flutter of her pulse. "But—but why should it take so long?" She watched as he put down the pot and served himself some strawberries. "Max?"

He looked up, his expression polite and pleasant—but she saw something unexpected in his dark eyes. Her pulse leaped nervously.

"What is it, Francesca?" he asked. His voice was soft, almost gentle.

She touched the tip of her tongue to her lips. "How long—how long have we been under way?"

He frowned as he glanced at his watch. "Let's see—it's almost eleven o'clock. I think we put to sea somewhere around six this morning."

She sank back in her chair. "You mean we've been traveling for five hours?" She took a breath. There was another question that had to be asked, but she was afraid to ask it. The best she could do was dance around its perimeter. "But that's impossible." Her lips turned up in the stiff beginnings of a smile meant to assure him that she knew he was joking. "How could it take us such a long time to reach Monaco? I mean, it was no trip at all by car..."

Max nodded. "You're right, of course. Monaco is a stone's throw from Nice." He bit into a strawberry, his teeth very white against the crimson fruit. "But Corsica is eight hours away."

She stared at him. "Is this a joke?" Her voice was steady, which amazed her, because every other part of her body was beginning to tremble. "Because if it is, it's not terribly funny."

He looked up. "It's not meant to be," he said quietly.

Oh, God. Oh, God. Oh——

Francesca clasped her hands together in her lap. "Take me back," she said.

"Back?" His lips drew away from his teeth in a cold smile. "Ah, yes. Back to your dear, beloved step-brother."

"You said——" She paused and drew herself together. "You said you'd have me back by sunrise. You said——"

Max tossed his napkin on the table and pushed back his chair. "Things have changed." His tone was flat, as flat as his eyes. "Look, you'll only make it harder on yourself if——"

"You never intended to take me back, did you?" Her voice cracked. "You intended this right from the beginning." She stared at him, wide-eyed, and then she exploded from her chair. "Well, you won't get away with it. Not with kidnapping! Your crew may have been willing to stand by while you carried an unwilling date aboard for dinner last night, but——"

"*My* crew," he said softly, his eyes on her face, "does exactly what I tell them to do." His mouth tightened. "Especially since they're all from Corsica."

"Corsica?" Her voice rose; she heard the hysteria lying just beneath the surface and she swallowed hard. "You say that as if—as if it's another planet."

His lips drew back from his teeth. "Some think it might as well be. Even the language is difficult for outsiders to understand."

"You make it sound exotic. But they speak Italian. And French—unless you're going to try and convince me that the chef you boasted about and Captain Dussage are Corsican."

"It doesn't matter a damn what they speak. My people are completely loyal." He gave her another wolfish smile. "And very romantic. Corsican men understand abducting a woman in the name of passion. When my crew realized what I was doing, they were more than eager to help."

Francesca clenched her fists. "You—you bastard! It wasn't enough that you made fools of Charles and me in front of everyone. No, you needed something more to soothe that insane ego of yours. You——"

Max's chair clattered to the deck. She fell back as he came swiftly toward her, but there was nowhere to go.

"How much do you remember of last night, *cara*?" His hands closed on her shoulders and he half lifted her to her toes. "Do you remember when I took you on deck to see the stars?"

"You took me on deck to get me drunk," she said with disdain.

A smile curved across his mouth. "You needed no encouragement from me. You drank the champagne as if it were water."

"If I did—*if* I did—it was because—because I needed it for courage."

"Ah." He laughed softly. "I see. You were afraid of me, hmm? You needed the wine to face me."

Her chin lifted. "Something like that, yes."

His arms slipped around her and he drew her unyielding body into his embrace.

"You needed no courage when we danced, *cara*." He bent to her and she tried to pull away but his mouth brushed her temple with fire. "I think you needed the courage you found in the wine to keep you from doing what you wanted to do."

Francesca's heartbeat stuttered. "This is insane."

She caught her breath as his lips pressed against her throat. "You wanted me to make love to you last night, and you were afraid."

"No!" She twisted uselessly against his strength. "Don't be ridiculous. I never——"

Max's hands clasped her head and held it still. "I asked you a question last night, Francesca. And you answered it. Can you recall?"

Remember it? She remembered it all, with painful clarity, his question and her answer, too. What if I had simply asked you to come away with me? he'd asked. Would you have come...? And she—she had said...

"Francesca?"

She drew a deep breath. "No. I—I don't remember."

A tight smile curved across his mouth. "Then I must refresh your memory." His hands held her fast when she tried to turn her face away. "I asked you what you would have done if I'd asked you to come away with me last night, before your stepbrother and I played out our foolish duel."

"I had a lot to drink, Max. I don't——"

"And you said..." His voice dropped to a whisper as his hands spread into her hair and tilted her head back. "You said you would have."

"I said that I might have. I never..." Color swept along her cheeks as he began to smile. "It doesn't matter," she said desperately. "It was the wine talking, not me."

"Was it?" He moved closer to her. She felt the warmth of his breath on her face. "You were like flame in my arms."

Her heart stumbled. "I just told you, it was the wine."

"It was the same the night we met, *cara*." He shifted his weight until his body was pressed lightly against hers, the heat of him threatening to ignite her. "Was it the wine talking that night, too?"

She stared into his eyes. "What—what do you want from me?" she whispered.

Max's eyes turned to smoke. "What if I said I was taking you to Corsica so that I could finish what began that night in the garden? What if I said I was going to make love to you until you'll never wish to run away from me again?"

What he was saying was crazy. She didn't want any of those things: Max Donelli was a stranger. No, he was less than that. He was Charles's enemy, and hers. He had made both of them look like fools, he had stolen from their corporation, and now he had abducted her.

And yet—and yet when he touched her, when he took her in his arms, the world spun away.

Francesca's breath caught. She felt as if she were trapped in a gallery of mirrors. Nothing was as it seemed, nothing could be trusted, and there was only one way to deal with such terrifying unreality.

"All this has nothing to do with me," she said in a shaky voice. "You hate my stepbrother, and you want vengeance. All the rest is just window dressing and we both know it."

Max's arms tightened around her. "Is it?" He gave a choked laugh. "Perhaps you're right, *cara*. But what does it matter so long as the outcome is the one fate has written for us?" He brought her closer and kissed her again and again, until her treacherous lips parted beneath his and her body began to quicken and then he drew back. "You will end up in my bed," he said in a low, harsh voice, "and to hell with the rest."

He looked at her for what seemed an eternity, and then he thrust her from him and strode away.

CHAPTER EIGHT

MAX'S words stunned her. Staring at his retreating back, Francesca wanted to shout, to run up to him and pound her fists on his shoulders—but she couldn't move so much as a muscle. Her legs felt as if they'd been caught in quicksand.

"Signorina?" She spun around to find Luigi standing beside her, his face set in a deferential smile, a fresh pot of coffee in his hands. *"Mi scusi,"* he said pleasantly. *"Posso lei dare ancora del caffè?"*

She stared at him incredulously. He was offering her fresh coffee, as if—as if she were a passenger on a pleasure cruise instead of a prisoner. The realization freed her, and she moved quickly toward the table and swept her hand across it. Coffee and cream spilled across the white linen; china and silverware clattered to the deck.

"Signorina!" Luigi looked at her as if she'd lost her mind.

"Get away from me," she spat, as he took a step toward her. "You just——" Abruptly, she spun away and ran toward the companionway.

By the time she reached the cabin deck, she was trembling as much with rage as with fear. The corridor was empty, the doors all were shut. Francesca took a deep breath.

"Max," she called. There was no answer. She waited, then shouted his name again. "Max, you bastard! Where are you? Damn you, where——?"

The door at the end of the passageway swung open. "I am not deaf, Francesca. What is it you want?"

"What is it I...?" She made a sound that was as much a sob as it was a laugh. "What I want," she said carefully, "what I *demand*, is that you tell your captain to turn this boat around and take me back to Monaco."

His hands went to his hips. "I told you, we are going——"

"To Corsica. Yes, I heard you. Well, now it's your turn to listen to me, Mr. Donelli." Her head lifted in defiance. "I don't know what you told my brother——"

"I told him nothing." The faintest of smiles curved across his mouth. "It was you who sent him a cable, *cara*. You explained that our meeting last night was not our first."

Francesca paled. "What?"

"Your cable told him we had met the prior night, at the Marqués's party. It mentioned——" his smile twisted wryly "—our strong attraction to each other."

"You told him about the incident in the garden?" She flicked her tongue across her lips. "But—but why?"

His smile grew sly. "Because I was sure you had not."

"Of course I hadn't. That was—it was..."

"Don't worry, Francesca. Charles will understand. Your cable made it very clear that you and I spent an extraordinary night together."

Two crimson spots appeared on her cheeks. "He won't believe you."

"And that we couldn't bear to be parted at dawn," he said, as if she hadn't spoken.

"Is that your scheme?" Her nostrils flared with distaste. "To get even with my stepbrother by making him think you and I have become lovers? It won't work, Max. Charles will never believe it. He'll know it's a lie."

He shrugged his shoulders lazily. "Perhaps."

"He will. And he'll notify the police."

"No, he will not." Max's smile chilled her. "The last thing your beloved stepbrother wants is publicity—especially if it involves his relationship with me."

Francesca's breasts rose and fell with the quickness of her breath. "You're so damned sure of yourself——"

"I'm sure about some things, yes. If I were not, I wouldn't have taken this course of action."

"Course of action?" Her voice dropped to a dangerous whisper. "Is that what you call this—this farce?"

"Everything will be done to make you comfortable, Francesca."

"Everything—except setting me free."

She had meant the words to sound angry. Instead, they seemed tremulous. The hard lines in Max's face softened a little.

"Are you afraid?" he asked.

"No," she said quickly. Too quickly. Even she could hear that her answer was a lie.

He walked slowly toward her. "You mustn't be," he said softly.

Francesca swallowed. "I told you, I'm not."

She was, though. Her heart was leaping like a frightened rabbit's. He looked at her while the seconds passed, and then he reached out and smoothed the hair back from her cheek.

"You're in no danger, *cara*. I promise you that."

She stared at him in disbelief. How could he stand there and make such a vow after what he had done to her? Did he think she was a fool—or did he think she'd fallen so far under his spell that she would accept any falsehood he uttered?

Tears welled in her eyes and she blinked them back.

"Do you seriously expect me to believe you?" she demanded in a husky whisper. To think that she had gone willingly into this man's arms, to think that she had ever been such a fool... "I wouldn't believe you if you—if you told me that the sun rose in the east!"

"Francesca, listen to me——"

"No." She struck away his hand as he reached out to her. "I'll never listen to you again. I'll never believe anything you say."

"Francesca." His hands cupped her face and lifted it to him. "I will not hurt you. You must believe that."

"No? Then why have you abducted me?"

Max went very still. "I—I have my reasons," he said finally.

"I just hope you know how much I hate you," she said tightly. "You're a—a crook and a thief. My stepbrother was right."

"Stop it. You don't know what you're saying."

She laughed shrilly. "What would you prefer me to call my kidnapper, Max? A prince among men?"

"You know nothing about me, Francesca."

"Oh, but I do. I know a great deal about you." She pulled free of him and stepped back, her chest heaving with emotion beneath the cotton shirt. "For instance, I know that I was wrong to call you a barbarian." Her eyes flashed dangerously. "Barbarians, at least, lived by some kind of code." Angry tears rose in her eyes again and she brushed her arm across her face and wiped them away. "What you are is—is an animal. A savage who lives by his own rules and doesn't give a damn for any——"

She cried out as he caught hold of her again, his hands digging into the tender flesh of her upper arms.

"That's enough," he said softly. "Don't say anything else or you'll regret it."

Her heart thudded with fear, but she had gone too far to stop now.

"Charles knew all about you."

Max's teeth showed in a feral smile. "Ah, yes. That precious stepbrother of yours. I'm sure he thinks as highly of me as I do of him."

"He said you couldn't stand losing. He told me that was why you hated him so much."

Max's face became grim. "Did he?"

"Charles did nothing to you. You're the one who stole from us."

His expression grew even grimmer. "Us," he repeated softly. "Yes. How foolish of me, *cara*. Sometimes I forget that you and he are partners. It's good that you remind me."

Francesca drew a deep breath. She had reminded him of too much, she thought, watching his dark face. What she should be doing was trying to talk her way out of this instead of angering him.

"Look," she said carefully, "why don't we just—just forget all about this? You can set me ashore some-where—it doesn't have to be Monaco—and I—I won't tell anyone what you did. I'll just..."

"What you'll 'just,'" he said coldly, "is do as you're told. Do you understand?"

"Max. Listen. I——"

He shook her. "Do you understand?" he demanded. The steel in his voice sent all her good intentions scattering.

"Or?" Her heart was thudding, but she looked straight into his eyes. "What will you do if I don't? Beat me? Tie me up? Toss me overboard?"

A cool smile curved across his mouth. "The first two ideas have possibilities," he said softly. His glance flicked over her face and came to rest on her mouth. "Relax, *cara*. My tastes run to far simpler pastimes. I can think of better things to do with a recalcitrant woman."

She felt the blood drain from her face. He stood looking at her while the seconds flew past and then, finally, he lifted his hands from her with exaggerated care and stepped back.

"I suggest you go to your cabin and get some rest. Maria will bring you a light lunch."

"I don't want anything to eat."

"The choice is yours," he said with a shrug of indif-ference. "I'll have her call you when it's time to go ashore."

"I don't want anything to eat, and I don't want to rest." He turned and began walking away from her. "I don't want anything from you or from your damned servants," she called as he opened the door to his cabin. "Do you hear me?" Her voice rose. "Max, damn you——"

The door swung shut after him. Francesca stood in the corridor staring at it, trembling from head to foot. Why was he doing this? Because he wanted her, he said, but it didn't ring true. He was right when he'd said he could have had her last night. The ugly fact was that each time he touched her the raging fire within him set her ablaze. But a man like Maximillian Donelli didn't kidnap a woman to seduce her—he wouldn't need to and besides, no matter what he said about the loyalty of his crew, the penalties—if he was caught—were terribly high.

Why, then? Why had he carried her off? She was certain it had something to do with Charles. But what could he hope to accomplish?

"Signorina?"

Startled, she turned and looked at Maria. The girl was smiling politely and holding a tray laden with covered dishes.

"I don't want anything," Francesca said coldly. *"Niente,"* she said, "is that clear? I don't want a damned thing from you or any of the other pirates on board this ship."

The girl's face fell as she swept past her, opened the door to her cabin, then slammed it shut resoundingly, the crash punctuating her frustration.

Trembling, Francesca fell back against the door and closed her eyes. She was caught in some kind of deadly game between her stepbrother and Max Donelli. She'd been a fool to think their private war had ended at the Casino. Their battle was like a game of chess. One player moved a piece forward, testing his opponent's defenses. The other countered with a move of his own, and she— she had had the misfortune to somehow have become a pawn that each man wanted to control.

Francesca drew an unsteady breath. Max had promised that he wouldn't hurt her. Despite all his lies, she wanted to believe him. But she played chess herself, just well enough to know something that made a lump rise in her throat.

Pawns were almost always expendable.

By midafternoon she was seated beside Max in a dusty off-road vehicle, clutching at the dashboard and trying her damnedest not to look over the side of the road where the cliff seemed to drop into the sea. They had been driving for what seemed forever, but she knew that not much more than an hour had passed since they'd docked in the harbor of a town with an unpronounceable name. Max had taken her arm and led her from the boat, and any thoughts she might have had of trying to escape him had instantly vanished.

"Don Maximillian!" someone had shouted. Within seconds, a small crowd of men had gathered around, all of them smiling and joking in a language that bore a resemblance to Italian as well as to French. Looking at the lined, weathered faces, hearing the strange accents, Francesca for the first time realized how very alone she really was.

Max heard her swift intake of breath. He looked at her, and she saw a sudden glint of compassion in his dark eyes.

"It will be all right," he said softly, slipping his arm around her waist.

She didn't question his ability to read her thoughts this time, nor did she offer more than token resistance to that hard, protecting arm that lay curved around her.

"Will it?" she whispered, as much to herself as to him.

"Yes," he said. "Trust me, Francesca."

Trust him? Trust her abductor? The concept was obscene, but what choice did she have? She was adrift in an alien world and Max was her only link to safety.

And so she'd stood quietly beside him, trembling like a skittish colt while he talked with the little crowd that had gathered. Someone must have asked about her; she had seen all the rough-hewn faces turn toward her. Max's arm had tightened around her, he'd said something that made them all smile, and then he'd led her down a narrow, cobblestoned alley to where a black Range Rover sat in the shadows.

"Buckle your seat belt," he'd said after he'd helped her into the Rover and climbed in beside her, but her hands had been shaking too much to work the catch. Max's arm had brushed lightly across her breasts as he leaned over and closed it for her, and then he'd turned on the engine and they'd driven through a maze of ancient streets until, at last, they had reached this narrow road that led into the mountains.

Now, as the road rose steeply in a dizzying series of switchbacks, Max looked over at her.

"The view from here is spectacular. You can see all the way down to the water."

She gave a quick, nervous glance out of the open window. The view was more than spectacular, it was terrifying, and yet they were still climbing. She could see the road snaking ahead, rising sharply up and up the mountain.

Where were they going? she wondered. To a village Max knew? That seemed likely. She had hoped they were heading for a city at first, but who would build a city in a place as wild and remote as this? And what was that scent in the air? It seemed a rich mélange of wildflowers and herbs; honeysuckle and thyme, perhaps, or lavender.

Francesca folded her hands in her lap. There were a dozen questions she wanted to ask, but you didn't sit and chat with your captor. You endured—and you looked for a chance to escape. She'd been paralyzed when they'd docked, too frightened at finding herself in strange surroundings to try and get away. Once they reached the village to which he was taking her, it would be different.

Her mouth turned down. People would probably rush to greet him there, too. The great *Don Maximillian* seemed to have quite a following. But the pleasure of his return would wear off after a few hours; she'd wait just long enough to get the lay of things, see who to approach, and then make her move. There'd be a mayor or a constable, someone in authority who would have to do something about Max's free and easy approach to kidnapping.

Her pulse quickened. And there'd be a telephone and, if she were lucky, an English-speaking tourist or two who'd wandered off the main path.

Max glanced over at her. "What are you thinking about, *cara*?" He laughed softly. "Never mind. I needn't have asked. From the look on that lovely face, I assume you're plotting your escape. Will I have to keep a twenty-four-hour guard on you, Francesca?" Amusement colored his voice. "Perhaps it will be best if I shackle you to a dungeon wall."

Her heart turned over. He wouldn't do such a thing—would he? Say something, she told herself, say anything just so long as you divert him from what he's thinking.

Francesca cleared her throat. "Actually," she said with great composure, "I was wondering if anyone lived up here except mountain goats."

Max laughed. "There are people here, as you'll see soon enough." He gave her a quick glance. "None who speaks your language, unfortunately."

Her jaw jutted forward. "Yes, I'm sure that breaks your heart."

He smiled as he swung the Rover into a tight turn. "This is not quite the sort of place you're used to, is it?"

She looked out of the window. The road dropped off sharply just beyond the wheels of the car, falling what looked like thousands of feet to the sea.

"No," she said with a little shudder, "it's not."

Max nodded his head. "It is a beautiful land, Francesca. Harsh, but beautiful."

She had to admit that he was right. There was a wild, almost primitive beauty to the countryside. It was, she thought suddenly, like the man seated beside her: hard, unforgiving, yet with a fierce, proud beauty that cut to the heart.

Francesca's fingers laced together in her lap. She was thinking nonsense. She wasn't here as a visitor, she was here as a captive, and nothing could change that. It was just that being a captive, alert for a chance to escape, made her aware as never before of everything she saw around her. Max's hard, tanned hands lying lightly on the steering wheel; his thigh flexing under its tight denim cover as he shifted gears; the musky male scent of him mixing with the odor of wildflowers drifting through the open windows. She had even noticed it when they were still at sea and the island was an indistinct mass rising from the ocean. It was like perfume, heady and rich and mysterious...

"Did you know they call Corsica the perfumed isle?"

She turned slightly and glanced at him. "I wish you wouldn't do that." Her voice had an edge to it.

"Do what?" He looked at her and a smile tilted at the corners of his mouth. "Only witches, warlocks, and the practitioners of the dark arts can read your thoughts, *cara.*"

"I don't know how you do it. And I don't much care. I just—I don't like it, that's all. It's—it's disconcerting to have someone play parlor tricks like that."

He gave her a slow, intimate smile. "Are you afraid of what secrets I might uncover inside that pretty head?"

She felt the rush of heat to her cheeks. "I told you, I don't like it. It's—it's unnatural."

"I'm sure it is." His smile took on a bitter twist. "But then we savages have such strange abilities, don't we?"

Another wash of color rose in her face. She stared at him in silence and then she twisted around in her seat and looked through the windshield.

"Are you going to tell me what that scent is, or must I guess?"

Max chuckled. "It's *maquis*—the shrubs that you see clinging to the mountain's slopes. It's a combination of a dozen kinds of vegetation: honeysuckle, lavender, rosemary and eucalyptus——"

And thyme." Francesca shrugged her shoulders when he looked at her. "I know the smell of thyme," she said. "I grow some in a little container in..." Her voice faded away when he looked at her.

"You grow thyme?" he said, as if she'd just admitted she raised chickens. "Where?"

"On the terrace." Her tone was defensive. "Lots of people have herb gardens in New York. Just because you've never heard of it——"

"And what do you do with the thyme you grow?" He glanced at her, amusement—or was it derision?— dancing in his eyes. "Do you, perhaps, package it for distribution to the homeless?"

Francesca drew herself up. "I use it," she said coldly, "in my cooking."

"On the cook's day off? How noble."

"I like to cook," she said, "and I'm quite good at it. Not that it's any of your business. As for the homeless, the only thing I package for them are sandwiches at the Henry Street soup kitchen."

There was a silence and then Max puffed out his breath. "So," he said softly, "the life of a débutante bores you, hmm?"

"What's the matter, Max? Doesn't that suit the image you've got of me?"

"It would seem that we know very little about each other."

Francesca turned away from him and crossed her arms over her breasts. "That suits me just fine."

He glanced across at her and grinned. "There's no television or radio where we're going, *cara*. I wondered how I would keep you amused, but this talk has solved the problem. We can fill the days by telling each other our life stories."

A lump rose in her throat. Days, she thought, days...

"Francesca? Are you all right?"

She swallowed hard. "I—I'm tired, that's all."

His mouth softened a little. "And you must be hungry. Maria tells me you refused lunch."

"I had no appetite."

He shifted his long legs beneath the dash. "Giulia will have something waiting for us, I am certain." He smiled. "I warn you, you must eat a bit of everything or she will be upset."

Giulia. Who was Giulia? She ached to ask, just as she ached to ask all the other questions that plagued her. But to ask him questions would be a mistake; it would only call attention to the fact that she was at his mercy.

"Once, just after Jean-Paul came to work for me, I made the foolish mistake of bringing him with me to Sarcene."

Sarcene. Was that where he was taking her, to a town called Sarcene? What kind of town would it be, perched high up in these dark mountains?

"...almost came to blows." Max chuckled. "Well, perhaps that's an overstatement. Jean-Paul is too much a gentleman. But Giulia was ready to kill him. 'He invaded my kitchen,' she kept saying, as if he were an *assassino* who'd broken into the castle." He grinned at the memory. "So now I maintain the peace by keeping Jean-Paul far from Sarcene. It's big, but not big enough for two cooks."

Not big enough for two cooks, but big all the same. Sarcene was a fair-size town, then. That was good. Francesca smiled to herself. Max might control the crew on *Moondrift*, but surely not all the citizens in Sarcene would owe their loyalties and their paychecks to the great

Don. The only person she'd have to deal with would be this housekeeper named Giulia, and, despite his having said that no Corsican would question his having carried her here, there was a good chance another woman might view her plight with some sympathy.

Her heart lifted. Things were looking up. They were definitely looking...

She blinked as they rounded a curve. "What is that?" she said.

Max slowed the car. He swiveled toward her, his eyes fixed to her face as she studied the stone walls and turrets that seemed to cling to the very top of the mountain.

"What does it look like?" he asked with faint amusement.

"It looks like—like a castle," she said slowly. "Like something out of a fairy tale."

"Yes." His voice was soft, almost gentle. "That is what I thought, too, when first I saw it. It is beautiful, don't you think?"

It *was* beautiful. It was also, Francesca thought uneasily, as forbidding looking a place as she had ever in her life imagined, standing in splendid isolation and overlooking the windswept slopes and the sea far below.

Max put his foot to the gas and the car moved forward.

"Who lives here?" Why did her voice sound so breathless? She ran her tongue along her dry lips. "Where are we?"

He paused just long enough so that she knew the answer before he gave it.

"This is Sarcene," he said quietly. "It is my home."

CHAPTER NINE

FRANCESCA stood at the narrow, arched window in her room, staring out over the neatly planted fields that stretched, unimpeded, to craggy mountain peaks on the horizon. It was late in the day, and very hot. Everything lay silent around her, caught in that heavy stillness that came in late afternoon in midsummer.

She watched as a bee lazily explored the dark green ivy that twisted up the stone walls of Sarcene, its movements languid and heavy. That was how she felt. She ached to lie down on the canopied bed that stood on the far wall, let her lids droop over her eyes, and sleep. But she had already tried that and it hadn't worked. As exhausted as she was, sleep eluded her. Finally she'd risen from the bed, come to this window, and thrown it open to the rich, sensual perfume of the *maquis* and the soft whisper of the breeze ruffling the sea of golden grass below her window.

With a sigh, she sank into the cushion-strewn window seat and curled her arms around her knees. A herd of shaggy, long-haired goats was grazing below the window, their collar bells tinkling softly as they moved across the meadow. In the near distance, a tractor crawled through a field of dark green vegetation.

This peaceful, pastoral view from her bedroom, so unlike that first glimpse she'd had of Sarcene, rising like a medieval fortress from the craggy mountain, had surprised her. Max had sensed it; he'd given her one of his cool, sardonic smiles and asked if she'd expected to see dragons instead of goats.

Well, who could have blamed her if she had? That initial sighting of the castle had not been encouraging. She sighed again and lay her head on her knees. Sarcene and its master were very much alike, when you came down to it. Both were studies in contrasts, dark and frightening one moment yet warm, even gentle, the next.

She sat up straight. What was she thinking? There was nothing warm or gentle about a man who'd carry a woman off. She was in Sarcene against her will, and she'd be damned if she'd let Max forget that for a moment.

She was tired, too tired to think straight, that was the trouble. The shock of walking into Sarcene's high-ceilinged entrance hall and stepping back half a dozen centuries to a time when a man could, indeed, carry a woman off and lock her away in a high tower, had been even more confusing than she was willing to admit.

The dark woods, tile floor, and faded wall hangings were authentic. Francesca had been an art student and she worked at a gallery that specialized in historical artifacts. But it was one thing to see a few such things purchased as objets d'art and quite another to step into a man's home and find yourself amid enough things to stock a gallery.

Max had heard her swiftly indrawn breath. "What is it?" he said, turning to her. A wry smile thinned his lips. "Don't look so panicked, Francesca. Sarcene isn't as primitive as it looks. I assure you, we have all the modern conveniences."

She shook her head, on the verge of telling him that he'd misunderstood, that she was entranced by what she'd seen, not repelled—but then she looked into his cool eyes and sanity returned.

No matter how handsome it might be, a prison was still a prison.

"Really? It certainly doesn't look it."

Max's hand closed lightly on her elbow. "I'll show you to your room. I'm sure you'd like to bathe and change your clothing——"

"Change it for what? You booked me on our little cruise rather suddenly, remember?" She gave him a chilly smile. "Or do you have a branch of Sak's Fifth Avenue tucked away in the hillside?"

He laughed. "Not Sak's, no, but I'm sure we can accommodate you. I instructed Giulia——"

"Don Maximillian! Ah, bene. Bene. Buon giorno, signore. Come sta?"

A plump, middle-aged woman dressed in black was bearing down on them.

"Giulia," Max said, smiling. He stepped forward and caught her by the shoulders, but not in time to keep her from making a little curtsy. The gesture, so deferential and old worldly, was somehow even more shocking than Francesca's first glimpse of Sarcene, and suddenly the full reality of what had happened hit home. I'm a million miles from everything that means anything to me, she thought, and before she could prevent it she made a muffled little sound of distress.

Max turned toward her. "Francesca? What is it?"

She stared at him. Whatever happened, she could not afford to let him know that she was afraid.

"I just—I was just thinking that—that it must be wonderful to be greeted this way." She forced a coolly mocking smile to her lips. "With such gestures of obeisance, I mean. I'd have thought that kind of thing went out of style a hundred years ago."

His face darkened, but not with anger. She saw, to her surprise, that he was embarrassed.

"You are wrong," he said stiffly. "It is not something I like at all. Giulia knows that, but old habits die hard here."

The woman said something in a swift, musical language that seemed neither French nor Italian. Max nodded and drew Francesca forward.

"Si, ecce la signorina. This is Giulia, Francesca. She will see to all your needs."

Francesca stared at the round, olive-skinned face. Giulia was smiling pleasantly, but what did that matter? She was no better than a jailer.

"Buon giorno, signorina. Io sono——"

Francesca swung away. "You said something about a bath and a change of clothing," she said, her voice sharp.

Max's mouth narrowed. He said something to the housekeeper, who whispered a response and glanced at Francesca before turning away and hurrying down the hall.

"Giulia apologizes if she has offended you," he said coldly. "I assured her that your enmity is reserved for me."

"But you shouldn't have." Francesca's eyes met his. "If she is part of your household, then I'm more than willing to despise her as much as I despise you."

Max's mouth twisted. "It is not wise to make enemies," he said softly.

"It's not wise to kidnap women," she answered, just as softly.

He stared at her and then he turned away. "I've had the tower room prepared for you."

The tower room. It had such a melodramatic sound to it that it should have been funny. But it wasn't; her heart seemed to stumble.

"How nice." Her voice was calm. "Just like the Hilton."

Max took her arm and led her up the wide staircase. "There's a private bathroom," he said, ignoring the gibe, "and a wonderful view. I'm sure you'll be comfortable."

"Would it matter if I weren't?"

Now, hours later, she could still feel the way his hand had tightened on her.

"Accept the inevitable," he'd said softly, "and it will go easier."

Did he really think she would do that? She turned away from the window and stared around the room. Max had not lied about any of what had awaited her, she thought grudgingly. The room itself was more than beautiful, it was magnificent, with exquisite wall hangings, a wide bed canopied in wine red velvet, and a massive stone fireplace. The connecting bathroom was modern and comfortable and stocked with every possible thing she might have needed. Bath oils. Colognes. Lightly scented powders. A cabinet filled with soft, oversize towels. A handsome antique silver comb and brush set.

Max had promised there'd be a change of clothing waiting and there was, but it wasn't the sophisticated leavings of the women he had surely brought to his isolated hideaway for romantic trysts over the years. Instead, she found lying draped across the bed an ankle-length, loose gown of finely woven wool in a pale shade of cream that skimmed her body gracefully from breast to ankle. There were shoes, too, a pair of soft leather thong sandals that tied at the ankles.

As for the view, it was more than wonderful, it was spectacular, with the golden fields stretching to infinity on one side and the dark blue Mediterranean on the other.

It was, all in all, a perfect setting. But it was still a cage, and she was a prisoner in it. A knot seemed to tighten in her belly. Nothing would make her forget that. Nothing...

Someone rapped lightly at the door. Francesca touched the tip of her tongue to her lips.

"Yes? What is it?"

The door swung open. *"Signorina."* Giulia's dark face and eyes were inscrutable. *"Mi scusi, signorina, ma è ora per la cena."*

It had to be time for dinner. The condemned ate a hearty meal, Francesca thought, swallowing a rush of nervous laughter, but she wouldn't oblige. She would eat nothing at Max Donelli's table.

"Signorina?"

Francesca nodded, squared her shoulders—and stood back in surprise as a maid entered the room with a laden tray and set it on a table near the window. She uncovered all the dishes, then scurried from the room.

"Buon appetito."

Francesca stepped forward just before the door swung shut again. "Wait..." The housekeeper turned, her brows raised in question. "The—the *signor*—isn't he—isn't he eating with me?" Giulia made a helpless gesture with her hands, and Francesca puffed out her breath. "Never mind. It doesn't matter. I just—I just wondered if—if..."

She broke off in confusion. What was wrong with her? It *didn't* matter. Max was leaving her alone on this first night at Sarcene. Well, that was good news—wasn't it? Of course it was. She didn't want to see him. She never wanted to see him again.

"Signorina? Va bene?"

Francesca looked at Giulia. She didn't have to understand the language to know that the woman's face was set in lines of concern and suddenly she felt embarrassed for having treated her with such contempt a little while before. She wasn't responsible for her employer's actions.

"Giulia." She hesitated. "I'm sorry for what happened when we met. Do you understand?"

The broad, olive-tone face softened. She put her hand out to Francesca, as if she was going to say something. After a few seconds, she sighed and lifted her shoulders in an expressive shrug.

Francesca smiled. "We'll just have to do the best we can, I guess."

Giulia touched her arm lightly, as if in agreement. *"Buona sera, signorina."*

Francesca nodded. "Good night."

She stood still after the door had shut, then walked slowly to the table and inhaled the tantalizing scents wafting from the serving dishes. Everything looked and smelled delicious, even the things she didn't recognize. Her stomach growled softly and she put her hand lightly against it.

She was hungry. Very. It would be silly not to eat something if she was dining alone. Anyway, what would not eating accomplish except to weaken her? She would need her strength if she was going to keep her wits about her and find a way to escape from Sarcene. Francesca drew a platter of cheese and fruit toward her. Yes. There had to be a way out of here and tomorrow she would set about locating it.

The resolution—and the food—made her feel better. Sarcene might look like a castle but there were no locked gates and she hadn't set eyes on any staff more imposing than the housekeeper and the maid. For the first time in hours, she felt a little rush of optimism. She would finish eating, climb into the canopied bed and get some much-needed sleep, and rise early, long before anyone expected her to. Francesca nodded to herself. With any luck at all, she would never have to see Max Donelli again.

She whimpered softly in her sleep.

"Francesca. What is it, *cara*?"

Someone was soothing her, stroking the heavy fall of pale hair from her face, feathering light touches across her skin.

Her eyes flew open. "Max," she whispered, even before she saw his face.

Yes. There he was, seated on the bed beside her, his hair lying ruffled on his brow, his chest bare above pale blue pyjama bottoms, his dark eyes fixed on her face. The sun was just rising—she could see its pale fingers touching the net curtains at the window beyond his shoulders—and its faint light tinged everything with an air of unreality. Even Max seemed unreal.

"Easy, *cara*." His voice was soft, hoarse with sleep. "You were having a bad dream."

She frowned, trying to remember, but the images were already fading. "I—I don't..." She hesitated. "What are you doing here?"

"I heard you call out. My rooms are just next door."

She stared at him. How could he have heard her, through walls as thick as these? It didn't seem possible, but how else could he have known she needed him? Unless he'd read her thoughts, as he had so many times before.

Her throat constricted. Needed him? What kind of nonsense was that? Why would she need the man who'd brought her to this place, who'd taken her from everything she knew and understood?

"Are you all right now?"

Francesca swallowed dryly. "Yes. Yes, I'm fine."

"Are you certain? Giulia tells me you were asleep by the time she returned for your dinner tray last evening."

"I was exhausted, that's all."

Max nodded. "Yes. I could see it in your face when I came to say good-night." He reached out and touched his finger to the high arc of her cheekbone. "Your eyes were dark with fatigue," he said softly. "And your lashes lie against your skin like bruises."

His words were whispers against her skin. Suddenly it seemed difficult to breathe.

"You mean—you came into my room while I was asleep? You had no right."

A little smile tilted at the corners of his mouth. "I told you, I wanted to say good-night—and apologize for not having joined you for dinner."

"It wasn't at all necessary. I was perfectly content to—— "

"Giulia thought you'd asked for me when she brought you your meal." He shifted his weight. "Was she right?"

He was so close to her now that she could see the intricate patterns made by the dark hair on his chest, smell the clean, masculine scent of his body.

"No," she whispered. It took all her effort to drag her eyes from his muscled shoulders to his face. "No. That wasn't—that wasn't what I asked her at all."

Max's hand stilled against her cheek. "What did you ask her, then?"

His voice was soft, as soft as the perfumed breeze that stirred the curtains.

"I asked—I asked her if—if..." Oh, God, why didn't he stop touching her? Her hands, hidden beneath the blankets, balled into fists as she fought against reaching out and—and... "I asked her if—if perhaps one of your other guests had—had left something behind that I could wear." She forced her eyes to his. "Something cooler than that dress, I mean."

He looked at her while the moments ticked away. "I'm sorry it didn't suit you, but it was the best Giulia could do on short notice. It belongs to her niece."

"I'm grateful for it. I only meant——"

"I know what you meant, Francesca. You meant to ask how many women have come to Sarcene before you."

"No." She spoke quickly. "That isn't it at all. What would it matter to me if you'd brought a hundred women to——?"

Max's fingers fell lightly across her mouth, silencing her. "I have never brought a woman here," he said softly. "You are the first, *bellissima*. You are the only one."

Her breath caught. I don't care, she wanted to say, it makes no difference to me whether I'm the first or the fiftieth...

But she couldn't say it, not while he was so close to her, not while his fingers lay across her mouth. She had only to part her lips if she wanted to taste his skin.

Time seemed to stop while Max looked at her. In the early morning silence that surrounded them, Francesca could hear the racing beat of her heart.

If he bent to her now, she thought dizzily, if he took her in his arms and kissed her...

But he didn't. He drew back instead and rose slowly to his feet. "Get dressed," he said. His voice was harsh, but she knew the tension in it had nothing to do with anger. "We will go to the market and buy whatever you need."

"Max?"

She whispered his name into the still air without even realizing she had spoken it. The single word was a question, an answer, a statement as old as the stone walls of Sarcene. His dark eyes swept over her, lingering on the silken hair spread across the pillow, the swift rise and fall of her breasts beneath the blanket, and then he muttered something under his breath that she could not understand and turned his back to her.

"Get dressed, Francesca. We will go to Corte." She saw the muscles in his shoulders and back roll as he took a deep breath, and then he stabbed his fingers into his hair, raking it back from his forehead. "And," he said in a low voice, "perhaps—perhaps we will talk."

Corte lay in the center of the island, high on the summit of a jagged mountain and surrounded on three sides by the mightiest of Corsica's rivers. A citadel, at least as old as any Francesca had ever seen in any Italian village on the mainland, dominated the town's ancient heart.

She had been quiet during the drive from Sarcene, wearing her silence like a suit of protective armor. What had happened between them this morning frightened her; her vulnerability to her captor had left her shaken and breathless. The best thing, she had decided as she sat in the car beside him, was to ignore him. She would say nothing, do nothing, simply endure his presence. It was what she'd promised herself from the start, and it was still good advice.

But by the time they were winding their way through Corte's narrow streets, Francesca's self-imposed silence had become a burden. She was bursting with questions, and, when she saw the citadel rise up before them, it was impossible to keep still any longer.

"What is Corsica?" she said suddenly.

Max glanced at her. "An island," he said, "as are most bodies of land surrounded by——"

"That isn't what I——" His laughter made her shift in her seat and glare at him. Her chin rose in defiance. "You know that's not what I meant."

"I know that you've been bursting with questions for the past half hour," he said calmly. "I only wondered how long it would take you to ask them."

She swung away from him and crossed her arms over her breasts. It was too late to keep quiet. Besides, what harm could there be in asking questions about the island? She might learn something that would help her make her escape.

"What is this place, then? The signs are all in French, but the language sounds as if it's Italian."

"It is." Max pulled the car to the kerb and shut off the engine. "Well, Genoese, anyway." He stepped out and came around to the passenger side. "Come. We'll find some shops and——"

"But the citadel is Spanish, isn't it?"

His brows arched in surprise. "It is, yes. That's quite a good guess."

Francesca shrugged. "It wasn't a guess at all. The arches and the stonework give it away."

He laughed softly as he put his arm around her shoulders. "For a woman who specializes in looking beautiful, you surprise me from time to time, *cara*."

She twisted free of his encircling arm. "What I specialize in," she said with taut dignity, "is art history. I have a degree in it."

Max looked at her. "Do you?" he said, as if she'd just told him she could read tea leaves.

"Yes." Her voice grew even colder. "I hope you didn't pay a fortune for the tapestries in my bedroom." She gave him a steady look. "They're not really Gobelins, you know. They're good. Very good. But——"

"But not Gobelins." He grinned as he put his arm around her shoulders again. It was a light gesture, meant only to guide her through the narrow, increasingly crowded streets, and she decided to ignore it. "No, they're not. They're seventeenth century, and not worth half what I paid for them. I knew that when I bought them, but I fell in love with the colors.''

She looked at him in surprise. "Did you?"

"Does that surprise you?" He smiled tightly. "That the barbarian should have a passion for art, I mean?"

Her face colored. "I didn't say that."

"You didn't have to." His voice softened. "You see? We still don't know very much about each other."

Her mouth felt dry. "We know all we need to know," she said stiffly.

Max's smile faded and, for just a few seconds, he looked at her as if they were alone in the world.

"No," he said quietly, "we do not." His arm tightened around her. "And I think, today, we will remedy that once and for all."

She tried not to fall into the trap he was setting, because it was a trap, she was sure of it. Whatever his game was, it involved getting past her defenses, changing her opinion of him little by little.

But somehow, as the hours passed, she found herself weakening, despite her determination not to succumb. The Max Donelli she'd glimpsed the night they'd dined together was back, and he was a man of great charm and easy conversation.

How could she not smile when he insisted she looked as pretty in the colorful cotton skirt and blouse she'd selected from a little market shop as she had in the gown she'd worn the night they'd met? She changed her clothing in a tiny room at the back of the little shop he'd taken her to; by the time she emerged, he was standing at the counter, his arms piled high with packages.

"What is all that?" she asked, and he smiled mysteriously.

"Things," he said and would say no more. But she knew he must have bought everything she'd so much as looked at; the sly smile on the face of the shopkeeper was a dead giveaway.

They loaded the packages in the car, and then set out on a slow walking tour of the city. Within minutes, Francesca was smiling again. Max was her tour guide, he said, and this was the Donelli Special. No professional guide, he insisted, could possibly sum up Corsican history as well as he.

"It's all quite simple," he said, smiling, but she saw a hint of sorrow in the smile. "Over the centuries, the island has been conquered by everybody. The Genoese, the Spanish——"

"And now?"

Max shrugged. "And now it's French." He smiled. "Well, its laws are French. But its heart is Corsican, and always will be."

"Like yours?" she said, watching him. "You told me you were born in New York City, but you're not really a New Yorker, are you?"

His teeth glinted in a quick smile. "No. I have a town house in Georgetown."

"But you weren't raised in the States," she said, "were you?"

Max shook his head. "My parents emigrated to America before I was born. But when I was fourteen my father died and my mother decided it would be best if she took me back to her family in Corsica."

Of course, she thought, that explained it. His accent, his way of dealing with things, as if he was a man with a foot in two cultures.

"And you prefer Corsica," she said softly.

He shrugged as he guided her to an outdoor café and seated her at a table beneath an umbrella. "This is a hard, unforgiving land," he said. "But there is a beauty to it, a wildness that will always hold my heart." He glanced up at the waiter who'd appeared beside the table. "Shall I order for you, Francesca?"

No, she thought, of course not. I'll order for myself.

But there wasn't time to say anything. He was already telling the waiter what they wanted, his hands as expressive as his voice. Francesca watched him from under the sweep of her lashes as he frowned over the menu. There was a wildness to him, too, the same wildness she had sensed before. A wildness as beautiful and as untamed as the land.

It was almost impossible for her to believe that she was seated at an outdoor café with a man wearing faded jeans and a navy cotton shirt, the sleeves rolled back along his forearms, obviously at home in a place that was as foreign to her as the moon. His skin was tanned, the color of wild honey, and his hair needed cutting, she thought idly. It brushed his collar each time he moved his head. She remembered how silken it had felt when she'd buried her fingers in it the last time he'd taken her in his arms and kissed her.

"So." His voice startled her. She blinked and looked at him. He was smiling, watching her through eyes as dark as the night. "What do you do with your degree in art history?" He smiled. "Besides check the provenance of the art work you stumble across, hmm?"

Francesca met his gaze steadily. "I didn't exactly 'stumble' across your tapestries," she said quietly.

Max's smile vanished. "No. You did not." He fell silent when the waiter appeared with a bottle of red wine. *"Va bene,"* he said, waving away the usual ceremony that went with opening the wine, just as he had at Stefan's café that first night.

Charles would have made a production of it, sniffing the cork and frowning while he sipped the liquid. The thought tripped into her mind without warning, and she shifted uneasily in her seat under the weight of its disloyalty.

"Max." Her voice trembled a little. He looked up and their eyes met. "You must take me back," she said quickly. "Just because you hate my stepbrother——"

"He stole from me, do you know that?" His mouth twisted as he leaned across the table toward her. "He bought the favors of a trusted employee, someone who knew the access code to my computer system, and with it he stole my client list."

"No." Francesca shook her head from side to side. "He wouldn't. He didn't. He——"

Max caught hold of her hand and held it tightly in his. "I could have survived that. But he stole the heart of my firm, Francesca, he stole my research and investment strategies." His face darkened. "Your stepbrother is a thief."

"No." The word was torn from her lips. Her chair clattered against the pavement as she pulled her hand free of his and struggled to her feet. "You're lying. Charles would never do something like that."

"Wouldn't he? Then, how did Spencer's suddenly become so successful?"

"Charles guided it. He made the right decisions..."

Max uttered a sharp, ugly word. "The only decision he made was to take that which was mine."

Tears rose in her eyes. "I see. And you—you decided to get even by—by taking that which was his."

She clapped her hand to her mouth, turned, and ran through the closely packed tables until she reached a narrow alleyway. Her footsteps quickened when she heard Max call after her. There was a square ahead; she could see the snarl of traffic, hear the bleat of horns. All she had to do was reach it, bang on a car door, scream for help...

She cried out as he caught her and spun her around to face him. "Let me go," she gasped. Her breath whistled in and out of her lungs as she pounded her fists on his chest. "Damn you, Max——"

His mouth slanted down hungrily on hers. She struggled against him, but it was useless. His arms went around her, gathering her to him; she fell back under his weight as he pressed her shoulders against the wall in the narrow alley.

When, at long last, he lifted his head and looked at her, she was shaking. Tears glistened in her lashes, then rolled down her cheeks.

"Francesca," he whispered. His hands slipped up into her hair, and he lifted her tear-dampened face to his. "Francesca," he said again, and she made a little sobbing sound deep in her throat.

"Damn you," she said fiercely.

But when he bent to her, her lips parted. Her arms wound tightly around his neck as she rose on tiptoe and crushed her body against his, and she kissed him and kissed him, as if she feared that this one breathless moment in time might never come again.

CHAPTER TEN

FRANCESCA had to escape. There was no other solution, short of becoming even crazier than she already was, for surely only insanity could have made her behave as she had in Corte.

Days had gone by but she couldn't stop thinking about it. The humiliating memory would come to haunt her when she least expected it—as it had just now, she thought as she rose unsteadily from her chair. There she'd been, sitting in the library, deep in a book she'd taken from the well-stocked shelves, and all at once the print on the page blurred and she found herself thinking of how she must have looked that afternoon, with her arms wound tightly around Max's neck, clinging to him as if she'd never want to be anywhere else.

Francesca made a little sound of impatience and blinked the image away. What had happened was simple enough to understand. She was his captive, she'd been under stress and she'd been disoriented. And then—and then, she thought grimly as she paced to the windows, there was the attraction she'd felt to Max when they'd first met. It was purely sexual—not a very comforting thing to admit to herself but true, just the same.

Sighing, she drew back the curtains and gazed out at the tranquil landscape. She understood that attraction, too. It had nothing to do with Max, it was just that he was so unlike the men she knew. He would never stand around at a cocktail party, making small talk so gossipy and banal that it made her ears ache just to listen. And he'd never come on to a woman the way the Marqués had, as if she were a mindless bit of entertainment to be had for the asking. Max was too proudly male, too elemental for such stuff. He would say what had to be

141

said, and to hell with the consequences. And he would tell a woman what he wanted, what he felt, and that woman would go to him gladly, eagerly...

Francesca closed her eyes and leaned her forehead against the glass. Yes, she thought, yes, she really did have to get away from here, and the sooner the better. She was coming apart, unraveling slowly but surely like the hem of a knitted sweater, and never mind that she hadn't seen Max for more than a few moments at a time since that afternoon in Corte—and she understood that, as well. The look on his face when the kiss had ended had said it all. He'd stared at her through cold eyes, just as he had the night at the casino when he'd watched the Marqués pawing her, and she'd known he must be thinking that she would give herself to any man if the situation was exciting enough for her.

I'm not what you think, she'd almost cried out, but sanity had prevailed and she'd choked back the words. Why did she give a damn what Max thought?

And yet—and yet, her heart ached when she remembered how he'd looked at her and the harshness in his voice when he'd finally spoken.

"It's getting late," he'd said, as if that moment of wildness between them had never occurred. "We must start back. The roads can be treacherous at night."

Inexplicably, her eyes had filled with tears. She'd have run off then, if she could have, but Max had read her thoughts again and his hand had clamped around her wrist, his fingers cold and hard as steel.

"Don't even think of it," he said grimly, and moments later they were seated in the car, moving swiftly away from the town and civilisation, into the silent countryside that surrounded them.

Francesca sat huddled in the corner of the car during the long drive to Sarcene, watching him, waiting for him to say something—anything—but Max never even glanced in her direction and finally she cleared her throat.

"You must let me go," she said softly. "Surely you see that."

He didn't answer. After a long time, she tried again.

"Max, for God's sake—what's the point to this? You can't——"

"Do you know what Corsica has given the world, Francesca?"

The question made no sense. But there was a darkness in his tone that made her wary.

"Napoleon," she said slowly, her puzzlement evident in her voice. "But that has nothing to do with——"

"The vendetta," he said abruptly. "The word is Corsican. Do you know what it means?"

"Yes," she'd said slowly, "I think so. It means—it means getting even with someone for something he's done to you."

His laughter had a bitter sound. "In the old days, it meant a blood feud, but as my countrymen became more civilized it became sufficient to recover one's honor without going quite as far as that."

Again, she felt the foolish sting of tears in her eyes. "And that's what all this has been," she said stiffly, "a vendetta against Charles. I knew that all the time."

The brakes screamed as Max stood on them and swerved to the narrow shoulder of the road.

"No," he snarled as the car came to a stop, "no, it was not. Despite what you think, Francesca, I am not a savage. This was—it was an opening move—a gambit."

"I don't understand," she whispered into the silence, and Max made a sound halfway between a laugh and a groan.

"There are those who cling to the old ways," he said, "who believe that what was done in the past was right. I never agreed. I always prided myself on being a man whose heart belonged to Corsica but whose mind belonged to the twentieth century. But now—now I wonder..."

Bewildered, she could only shake her head. Max stared at her for what had seemed a long time, and then he reached across the seat to her, cupped her face in his hands, and kissed her, so tenderly and gently that she was incapable of doing anything but giving in to the sweet seduction of his lips.

She heard the shuddering hiss of his breath when he finally moved away from her.

"I can't let you go, *cara*," he said in a voice as soft as his kiss. In the fading light of evening, his face had suddenly seemed white and drawn. "But I make you a promise. I will not bother you any more."

Why did his words make her tremble? "What—what do you mean?"

Max took a deep breath. "When we reach Sarcene," he said, his hands tight on the steering wheel, "I will give my people orders that you are to be allowed the run of the place."

"You mean——"

"I mean," he'd said, his voice turning cold, "that you may walk the grounds, use the library, anything you like——" The car had skidded onto the road as he stepped down hard on the gas. "Someone will always accompany you, of course."

Francesca had felt a sudden, terrible weariness. "Of course," she'd said, putting her head back against the seat.

"But it will not be me. I have—I have things to do while I am at Sarcene, too many of them to spend my time being with you. Do you understand?"

No, she hadn't understood, she thought now as she leaned back against the library wall. Not all of it, anyway, only enough to know that she had to find a way to escape Sarcene and Max Donelli before it was too late, or she would be lost forever.

"*Signorina?*" Startled, Francesca turned to face the door where Giulia stood, smiling politely. "*Desidera una tazza di caffè?*"

Francesca shook her head. Coffee, she thought with a sad little smile, the universal panacea. "No, thank you."

The housekeeper held out a folded note. She took it, her fingers moving lightly over the heavy vellum paper. She didn't have to read it, she knew what it would say. She hadn't seen Max since that day they'd returned from Corte; instead, he sent her these polite little messages. "Do you need anything?" he wrote. "Are you comfortable? I'm sorry, but there is much to do on the estate. I'm afraid I'll be gone for breakfast—and lunch and dinner."

"*Grazie,*" she said.

Giulia's black eyes softened. "*Signorina? Come sta?*"

Francesca nodded. "*Sono bene, grazie.*"

The housekeeper smiled. "*Lei parla molte bene.*"

Francesca smiled, too. You speak well, Giulia had said. If she'd made any progress it was because it was easier to attempt learning the language spoken at Sarcene than to spend her days living on hatred. And hatred was what she felt for Max, pure and simple. She despised him, and never mind that she kept hoping for a glimpse of him, that she kept remembering that kiss, that one dizzying kiss in Corte.

She moved toward the window and stared through the glass. It was a beautiful day, the sun hot, the sky a perfect blue, the golden fields ruffling like the ocean under the perfumed breeze. A lump rose in her throat. Charles had wanted to buy a caged bird once, some rare and exotic feathered jewel that cost a small fortune. Only the best people in New York could afford them, he'd boasted, but one look at the creature sitting in its ornate cage had made Francesca shudder.

"Nothing should live that way," she'd said, and she hadn't backed down, even in the face of Charles's irritation.

That was how she felt now, she thought, like a creature trapped in a cage. Maybe that was why she kept thinking about Max. Weren't captives supposed to form bonds with their captors? That would explain it all. That would...

She went very still. Far in the distance, a man rode across the golden field on the back of a night-dark stallion, its head angled as proudly as that of its master.

Francesca's heart turned over in her breast. Max, she thought. Max. She stepped back, although she knew he couldn't possibly see her. The net curtains protected her, and anyway the sun would be in his eyes.

Her blood slowed, thickened. She could hear it beating against her eardrums along with the silence of the hot, still afternoon. Her hand flew to her mouth as the horse stopped and the rider turned his head until he was looking at the castle.

He can't see me, she told herself again. I know he can't.

And yet—and yet she could feel those dark eyes on her. She could hear his voice inside her head. Come to me, *cara*, he said, come to me.

She stumbled back from the window and collapsed into a chair. Her hands shook as she put them to her face. She sat there for a long time, taking steadying breaths, willing herself to stop trembling. Maybe she really was going crazy. Maybe——

The door slammed open. She looked up, heart racing, and her eyes met Max's.

"Giulia tells me you are bored."

Her throat worked. "I—I am, yes," she said when she trusted herself to speak. Her chin lifted. "Despite what you may think, I'm not used to doing nothing all day."

He nodded. "What can I say?" He smiled coolly. "I told you that Sarcene was isolated. No television, no newspapers, no concert halls or balls or cocktail parties——"

"I offered to help with dinner last night," she said, as coldly as he. "But Giulia was horrified."

Max laughed. "I would think so. She has little need for the services of one for whom cooking is a chic hobby."

He made it so easy to hate him. She could, at least, be grateful for that.

"Are you always so damned sure of yourself?" she asked tightly.

The easy amusement faded from his face. "No. Not always." He shifted his weight and lounged back against the jamb, his arms crossed over his chest in that arrogant way he had. "I wish I could help you, but I can't. What could a woman with your skills do in a place like Sarcene?"

Her face blazed with color but she refused to rise to the bait. "I could catalog your books," she said stiffly. "Don't look so startled, Max, I've done it before. The gallery bought out the Bennett estate last year and I did the work on first editions."

His expression didn't alter. "Did you?" he said tonelessly.

"Yes." She put her hands on her hips. "I don't suppose you've had anyone inventory the furnishings here, either."

This time, his lips twitched. "The phoney Gobelins, you mean? No, no, I haven't."

"Well, you should. Those tapestries are valuable, even though they're copies. And there's other stuff, silver pieces and furniture and china..."

"You have been busy, then, exploring Sarcene."

"Always under the watchful eye of someone. Giulia, or Paolo, or Gianni."

"I hear that you've learned to speak some of our language."

"What if I have?" Her eyes flashed. "Is it forbidden for an outsider to try and fit into Sarcene?"

His teasing smile faded again and he gave her a long, searching look. "No," he said at last, "it is not forbidden. But it is unusual."

She tossed her head. "Perhaps it's because you won't let anyone fit in," she said. "Has that ever occurred to you?"

There was an even longer silence, and then he leaned away from the door.

"Do you ride?"

She stared at him. "Ride?"

"Horses," he said. "Do you?" She nodded, and he slapped his hand against his thigh. "Change into something suitable and meet me at the stables."

Her heart began to race as he turned away. With a horse beneath her, she might have a chance to escape. But her voice was steady when she called after him.

"Your thugs won't let me out the door."

He didn't even break stride. "They are my men," he said over his shoulder. "And they will do as they are told."

She had not ridden in years, not since boarding school, and she had almost forgotten how she loved it. The knowledge came as soon as she stepped into the stables and drew the rich, once-familiar scent of hay and horse deep into her lungs.

She watched as Max led a delicate Arabian from her stall to the paddock.

"She's gentle," he said, stroking the long, arched neck, "but she is spirited. Do you think you can handle her?"

She ran her hand along the Arabian's flank, then swung into the saddle. "I'm not afraid of things with spirit. I like that quality."

Max smiled a little. "Yes," he said, "as do I."

She tried to be alert to every chance for escape, but it was soon obvious that there were no roads or houses in the distance. And, after a while, it was hard to concentrate on anything but the feel of the horse under her, the warmth of the sun—and Max, riding along beside her. They had been apart for days, and she had missed him, she had missed his cocksure attitude and his sense of humor, his dark eyes and his sensual mouth, she had missed everything about him.

He looked at her and smiled. "What are you thinking, *cara*?"

Cara. It was so long since he'd called her that.

Francesca smiled back at him. "I was—I was wondering what grows in those fields. The grass is such a lovely golden color."

His smile broadened. "Wheat. And there is barley, too, and oats."

"This is really a working farm, then?"

He laughed softly. "It is now. It's taken a long time to get the soil to produce. It's been played out, over the centuries." He clucked to his horse as they made their way slowly up a hill.

"Has it?" she said in surprise. "But surely land that supports all the wonderful plants of the *maquis*——"

Max shook his head. "The *maquis* only grows where the soil is the poorest, *cara*."

"I can't believe it. How could something so beautiful take root in such a hard place?"

He looked at her. "I have wondered that myself," he said softly. "I suppose it is a kind of miracle."

It took all her strength to look away from his searching gaze. "Tell me—tell me about Sarcene. Did you inherit it from your father?"

"I wish I had." He smiled ruefully. "It would be nice to think that he had owned even a little piece of this island that he loved so dearly. But he did not. It has always been hard to earn a living in Corsica. My father was poor. That was why he and my mother went to America."

"Then why did she come back after he died? If it was hard to earn a living here, I mean?"

"I wondered, too, for a long time." He glanced over at her as they reached the top of the hill. "And then, one day, I understood. She came back because Corsica was all she had left of my father. Can you understand?''

Yes, she thought, oh, yes, she did understand. A fierce, bittersweet yearning rose up within her, constricting her throat so that it was suddenly hard to breathe. If you loved a man with all your heart, so that he became the very center of your universe, what would you have left if you lost him? Your world would be barren; you would do whatever you could to keep the memory of him and his love alive...

God. Oh, God...

"We can see all of Sarcene from that meadow. Would you like to ride there?"

Francesca blinked. Max was pointing to a gentle plateau covered in wildflowers. "Yes," she said, her voice trembling a little. She managed to smile at him. "I'd like that."

He was right, she thought, as the horses came to rest knee-deep in the sweet-smelling blossoms, you could see the whole world from here, or at least you could see all the world that mattered—Max and Sarcene. He swung down from the saddle, looked up at her, and held out his arms.

The breath caught in her throat. How could she have let this happen? How?

"Cara?"

She hadn't. The truth was that nothing she could have done would have kept this from happening. Max had spoken of fate when they'd first met. Fate would bring her into his bed, he'd said—but she had never dreamed that fate would make her fall helplessly in love with him.

Tears stung her eyes. It was such a simple, swift realization; the only thing that surprised her was that it had taken her so long to admit the truth to herself. What she'd felt that day in Corte wasn't hatred, it was love. She loved Max, loved him with a passion so all-consuming that she was certain it must be written on her face.

"Francesca. What is it?"

"I—I..." She shook her head and pressed her heels into the Arabian's flanks. She had to escape now, not just from Sarcene but from Max, from what she felt.

But he was too quick. He caught the horse's bridle, and then he was reaching up to her, his arms were closing around her, and he lifted her down from the saddle, her body sliding the length of his as he lowered her to her feet.

"*Bellissima,*" he whispered. His hands framed her face. "Ah, Francesca. My beloved."

Beloved. It was a word a man would use when he wanted a woman, it didn't have any real meaning. Or did it? Did she dare hope? Did she dare...?

"Max," she whispered, and she stopped thinking and went into his arms.

He kissed her windblown hair, her sun-warmed temples, her damp eyelids, and he whispered words of desire, words that excited and inflamed her, words that said he needed her, that he wanted her with a passion that was the equal of hers.

And, in his arms, in the blazing heat of his kisses, she let everything slip away, the questions and doubts, the darkness that had kept them apart. Destiny had brought them here and who was she to defy it? Standing on that hilltop, with the man she loved in her arms and the scent of the *maquis* all around them, Francesca knew that nothing in her life would ever matter as much as this moment.

She groaned as Max's hands slipped under her shirt and began moving over her. His touch was possessive, almost harsh, and she felt her body coming alive under it.

"Yes," she whispered as he cupped her breasts, "yes, touch me. Please touch me."

"I have wanted you for so long, *cara*." His mouth crushed down upon hers, driving the breath from her. "I want you now," he said thickly. "Here, in the sunlight." He pulled her shirt over her head. "You are so beautiful," he said. She cried out when he feathered his fingers across her nipples. Her head fell back as his mouth closed around her waiting flesh. Sensation blossomed low in her belly and a wave of heat raced through her body to center where his lips enclosed her. "So beautiful," he whispered. Her jeans slid down her legs and then her briefs, and she was naked before him.

Max stepped back and looked at her, his eyes as hot as the sun. She had wondered what it would be like to stand this way before a man. Would she be embarrassed to let a lover see her this way? Would she be frightened?

There was no embarrassment, no fear, there was only a heady rush of excitement as she watched Max's face. His eyes moved over her slowly, making her blood run hot under her skin. His hand caressed her breasts, her gently rounded belly, and her flesh came alive.

"Am I?" she whispered. "Am I beautiful, Max?"

"You are perfect, *cara*," he said. "Everywhere. Your face, your mouth." His eyes locked with hers as he touched her. "Here," he said, stroking her breasts, "and here."

She cried out as his hand moved over her, and then he dropped to his knees and buried his face in the pale golden curls at the juncture of her thighs. She moaned and swayed backward; she would have fallen if he hadn't caught her and held her still while he tasted her. Her face tilted up to the sun, her fingers clutched his dark, silken hair and she gave herself up to the fierce, abandoned joy of his caresses. When she sobbed his name, Max rose to his feet and cupped her shoulders in his hands. His kiss was deep, and the taste of their mingled passion and desire bloomed on her tongue.

"*Cara.*" She looked into his dark eyes as he drew back. "Undress me," he whispered.

Her hands trembled as she undid the buttons of his shirt. She heard him catch his breath as her fingers slid under the soft cotton and began learning the satiny feel of the dark hair that curled on his chest and the taut underlay of muscle and bone beneath his skin. He whispered her name as her hand drifted to the waistband of his jeans; she opened the button and paused, her heart thudding as she placed her hand lightly over the heavy weight of him that lay beneath the closed zipper. His body pulsed under her touch, and her heart leaped to match its rhythm.

Max groaned. "Wait," he said thickly as his fingers curled around her wrist and stilled her hand. His face was a mask of controlled tension. "Wait, *cara*. Slowly is the best way."

But she had waited too long. Days. Weeks. A lifetime—and she was done with waiting. She wanted him, she wanted to belong to him, she ached for the moment his body would conquer hers.

Her hand slid beneath his open waistband. "Make love to me, Max," she said. "Make love to me now."

He caught her hair in his hands and bent her head back, kissing her mouth and throat, and then, within seconds, his clothing lay discarded beside hers. There was only time to look at him and think, with wonder, that she had never imagined anything as beautiful as this hard, male body and then Max had her in his arms and he was taking her down, down into the soft grass and the wildflowers.

At the last moment, the moment before he filled her with his silken heat, Francesca remembered that she had not warned him of her innocence. She felt a second's trepidation, not of the pain of his possession but of what he might say when he realized she was not the sophisticated woman he had thought her to be.

But she should have known. He knew all her secrets. Why would he not have discovered this most private one? She felt the tension in his muscles as he held back from the ultimate sweet victory.

"Francesca." He lowered his mouth to hers and kissed her. "I won't hurt you, *cara*," he whispered. "I swear, I'll never hurt you."

The words made her want to weep. Yes, she thought with sudden terrible clarity, you will. You will.

But the time for thinking was past. Max was sinking into her, losing himself in her softness. Her body opened to him, folded around him, and he was moving, stroking, taking her with him on a journey that went beyond the stars, a journey that had begun the first night they'd met, and nothing mattered but the incredible joy of what was happening.

I love you, Max, Francesca thought, I'll always love you, and a moment later she was lost in the shattering explosion that consumed them both.

She awoke in his arms. He was asleep, his head cradled on her breast. She smiled as she watched him, the dark sweep of his lashes against his tanned cheek, the mouth that could be so demanding and yet so sweetly gentle. The sun had dropped toward the horizon; they had been here for hours, she thought, flushing with pleasure when she remembered how they had made love again and again before Max had finally chuckled wickedly and tucked her into the curve of his arm.

"Are you trying to kill me, you shameless Jezebel?"

She'd given him a teasing smile. "What if I were?" she'd said, and Max had given her a long, deep kiss.

"I would gladly die in your arms, *cara*," he'd said, and then he'd kissed her eyelids shut and they'd drifted off to sleep.

Her smile faded. Would a man say such a thing unless he loved a woman? Would he whisper the things Max had whispered to her, would he make her feel as Max had made her feel?

But there was still a question unanswered. Why had he carried her off?

"*Cara.*"

Her eyes flew to Max's face. He was awake, watching her with a heavy-lidded intensity that made her heart turn over.

"I—I think we should start back," she said. "It's getting late."

He smiled slightly. "Soon."

"Max——"

He rolled her beneath him. "Soon," he said again. "After I have done this——" She cried out softly as he touched her. "And this."

"Max. Oh, God, Max——"

"And this."

Her body arched up to meet his and she was lost— but she didn't know quite how lost until they were dressed and riding slowly down the dirt road that led to Sarcene. Suddenly, a car appeared heading toward them, emerging from a cloud of dust like an apparition. Its horn blared loudly and Francesca's horse shied. Max cursed, grabbed for her reins, and managed to steady the terrified animal.

The car door swung open and a man stepped out. *"Mi scusi,"* he began, but Max had already swung down from his saddle and was stalking toward the car. He let loose a blistering torrent of Corsican. When it ended, the man smiled nervously. Francesca could see his throat working up and down.

"Mi scusi," he repeated unhappily, *"ma io—io no comprende..."* He bent and peered into the car. "Agnes," he hissed, "where the bloody hell is that Berlitz?" A woman's voice whispered in response. He straightened up and tried the same nervous smile. "I really am sorry," he said. "But we were looking for this little village we'd read about, and the damned map seemed to show a turn-off a few miles back..."

Max took another step forward. "What the hell are you doing on my land?"

The man let out an audible sigh. "You speak English," he said with relief. "Well, thank goodness. Look, it's all a mistake. My wife and I went off on our own—we probably shouldn't have—we were looking for Gaspare——''

"You could have killed someone, you fool, do you realize that?"

"I'm sorry—I said I was, didn't I? Just tell me where Gaspare is, and I'll——''

"Turn back to the main road," Max said roughly. "Go south ten kilometers and look for a signpost. You can see the church steeple from there."

The man nodded. "Fine, fine. Thank you very much." He climbed back into the car, threw it in gear, then hesitated and peered out of the window. "Is that castle back there yours?" Max didn't answer. "If it is, the wife and I would love to get a look inside. We'd be willing to pay for a tour, of course."

Max stalked toward the car and slammed his fist on the roof. *"Basta,"* he roared. "Enough! Get off my land before I have you shot!"

The tires squealed as the car shot into Reverse, then bucked forward and changed directions. A rooster tail of dust rose in the air as it barreled down the narrow road and disappeared.

Max swung back toward Francesca. "Are you all right?" he demanded.

"Yes," she said, "of course. I'm fine. But that poor man..."

"That poor man," he growled, "could have killed you, *cara*." He strode to her and clasped the pommel of her saddle. "Had you fallen——''

"But I didn't," she said gently.

"No thanks to that—that idiot!" He went on glowering for a moment, and then he lifted his hand and lay it against her cheek. "Nothing must happen to you," he said softly. "Do you see?"

Francesca turned her face and pressed her mouth to his palm. "Am I so important to you?" she whispered.

His eyes grew dark and still in his face. "You have been, Francesca. From the very beginning."

His words made her heart fill with joy, but before she could respond he turned abruptly and swung into the saddle.

"It's getting late," he said. She watched as he tapped his heels into the Arabian's flanks and moved out into the road ahead of her. "Come," he said, "we will ride back to Sarcene."

Was there a sudden heaviness in his voice? Francesca urged her horse forward until she was abreast of him.

"Max? Is something wrong?"

"No," he said quickly, "no, of course not." He gave her a quick smile. "I just don't enjoy being waylaid by a horde of tourists."

Francesca laughed. "Two bewildered people aren't exactly a 'horde,' Max. Surely you can see——" She broke off, stunned, her smile slipping from her face. Two people, she thought, two people who spoke English. English! All she'd had to do was cry out, tell them she'd been kidnapped, that she was being held against her will, that she needed help...

"Francesca?"

She blinked. They had reached the stables, and Max had already dismounted. He was holding on to her horse's bridle, looking up at her, a question in his eyes. He held his arms up to her, his smile tilting crookedly, when she seemed to hesitate.

"*Cara,*" he said quietly. "Will you come to me?"

What if I had simply asked you to come away with me? Would you have come?

Her throat closed and it was in that one instant that she knew that she was, indeed, lost.

"Yes," Francesca whispered, looking deep into his eyes, "yes." And she leaned down, put her hands on Max's shoulders, and went unreservedly into his arms.

CHAPTER ELEVEN

FRANCESCA was in a large, brightly lit room, without furniture and without shadows, standing midway between Max and Charles.

"Would you have come with me?" Max kept saying.

Charles stood silent, motioning her toward him. But she couldn't respond to either of them. Her lips wouldn't move, her feet were rooted to the floor.

"You must choose, Francesca," Charles said.

"She has chosen," Max said, and she had. She had chosen him, but she couldn't tell him that, she couldn't get her throat to work...

She came awake with a gasp, her body jerking as she escaped the suffocating illusion, disorientated as much by the unfamiliar room as by the dream. Her pulse raced; she forced herself to lie still and take shallow breaths until her heartbeat slowed, became a steady counterpart to the distant beat of the sea on the rocks.

She was in Max's room. A flush rose along the length of her body. She was in Max's bed, and she'd spent the long, sweet night in his arms.

Her eyes opened slowly; a smile curved across her mouth as she turned her head on the pillow, anticipating that first glimpse of his face. But she was alone: his pillow still bore the imprint of his head, but Max was gone.

Francesca's gaze went to the closed door of the connecting bath on the opposite side of the enormous room, and she let out her breath. He was in the shower, then. She could envisage him standing inside the smoky glass shower stall, his strong body naked under the spray, his face turned up to the water, daring it to beat him into submission.

Her heart thudded foolishly. She knew how he must look, because they had showered together only yesterday, after they'd stabled their horses and returned to the castle.

"Where are you going?" Max had asked when she'd started toward her own bedroom.

Suddenly, she'd felt unaccountably shy. "I have to shower," she'd said, and he'd smiled and told her that sounded like a perfectly fine idea. The next thing she'd known she'd been in his bedroom, trembling as he'd stripped away her clothing and carried her into the shower stall.

"Let me bathe you, *cara*," he'd whispered, and he'd soaped her body slowly, then rinsed it with exquisite care, making love to her with each brush of his hands until finally her legs had trembled and she'd cried out his name and moved into his arms, her face pressed against his chest, her mouth open to the taste of his wet skin.

"*Beloved,*" he'd whispered, kissing her and kissing her, and then he'd lifted her to him, entering her with a swift, deep thrust. A soft, sobbing cry had burst from her throat and she'd come almost immediately, waves of sensation pouring through her muscles and nerves while the water streamed down their joined bodies.

I love you, Max, she'd thought, just as she had in the wildflower-filled meadow, but she'd kept silent, kept the words from spilling from her lips because even in that moment of ecstasy a treacherous voice inside her whispered that he had still not said the things that needed saying, that she didn't yet know what he felt for her or what his purpose had been in bringing her to Sarcene.

To her horror, tears had risen in her eyes. You're not a child, she'd told herself firmly, you know that making love and being in love don't always go hand in hand. He wants you. He cares for you. Isn't that enough? Just because you've fallen in love with Max doesn't mean— doesn't mean . . .

Max had put his hand under her chin and lifted her face to him. "Francesca? What is it?"

"Nothing," she'd said. "I just—I have soap in my eyes."

He'd smiled then, saying that she needed someone to look after her, and he'd wrapped her in a huge towel and dried her slowly, from head to toe, and by the time he'd finished, his hands and mouth had replaced the towel and she was clinging to him again, whispering words as heated and intimate as his.

Now, lying here with the morning sun streaming into the room, Francesca sighed and let herself relax into the softness of the silk-sheeted bed. She thought of the dream that had awakened her. As fuzzy as it had been, there was no denying the end of it. She *had* chosen, and not just in the dream. She knew now that what Max had said about Charles must be the truth. She still didn't know all of it, but she knew that Max Donelli was not a man who would lie, cheat, or steal. He was a man of honor—and she loved him.

Yesterday had changed everything, and last night had been a night of joy and wonder, a banishing forever of the bitterness and anger that had separated them. They'd dined by candlelight on the garden terrace and talked for hours, learning things about each other. Max had a passion for American football; she was certain the game was an excuse for legalized mayhem. He liked milk chocolate; she adored dark. Both of them loved classical music. Anything written after 1900, Max had announced sternly, had to be decadent.

Francesca told him how she'd felt when she was sent away to boarding school at the age of eight, just after her father's death.

"But how could your mother have done such a thing?" Max had demanded, with such anger that it had warmed her heart.

"I suppose I understand it now," she'd answered. "She needed to get her life together again."

"And did she?"

She had started to answer, to tell him that her mother had met Augustus Spencer a year later—and then she'd realized that mentioning her stepfather would only lead to Charles. Her stepbrother had no place in this conversation. He had no place between them at all, any more. All that was done with.

And so she'd simply smiled. "She did, eventually. What about your mother? Was she happy here, in Corsica?"

"I think so, yes. She missed my father, but she had friends."

And she had you, Francesca had thought, watching his face. What more could anyone ask than that?

They'd talked for hours, laughing easily and often, touching each other on the flimsiest excuse, until the crescent moon had risen high in the dark sky, and then, suddenly, the laughter and the talk had stopped.

"I want to make love to you, *cara*," Max had said in a husky whisper.

Her answer had been in her eyes. He had kissed her and kissed her while the stars blazed overhead, and then he'd swung her up into his arms and carried her into Sarcene while she'd clung to him tightly, her face buried against his throat, his footsteps echoing down the quiet halls and up the ancient steps. He had brought her to this room, to this bed, and they had made love until the moon slipped into the sea.

Francesca's lips tilted in a soft smile. Nothing that had happened had been what she'd expected. There was pain, some women said, but she'd felt only pleasure. There hadn't even been any blood, and yet she was sure Max knew he had taken her virginity. She'd been so shy, and yet so eager to learn—and finally, finally, Max had drawn her back tightly into the curving heat of his body, his hand splayed possessively across her belly, and she'd fallen into a deep sleep.

She sat up in bed, stretching luxuriously, the sheet and soft cotton blanket falling to her waist, and looked toward the closed bathroom door. Max was still showering. A little smile tilted at the corners of her mouth and she pushed back the covers, got to her feet, and pulled on the robe that lay tossed across the foot of the massive bed.

She would join him, under the water, she thought as she padded across the floor. She'd enter the room quietly, step free of the robe and into the stall. Her mouth felt dry as she opened the door. He'd be surprised when he felt the press of her breasts against his back...

Francesca's brow furrowed. The bathroom and the shower stall were both empty. Max wasn't here.

Where was he, then? Had he gone for coffee? He must have. He wouldn't have left her alone, not this morning, not after——

Her face cleared when she heard the bedroom door open. "Max," she whispered, and she turned and flew into the other room. "There you are," she said, with a radiant smile. "I wondered where you——"

"Buon giorno, signorina."

It wasn't Max, it was the maid, bearing a tray on which there stood a coffee service, trying, with no great success, not to look at the bed and its tangled sheets.

Francesca felt a dark flush rise into her face, knowing how she must look with her hair tumbled around her shoulders, her bare feet peeping out from beneath the hem of Max's robe, and the rumpled bed standing like a stage set behind her. But it didn't matter. She wasn't ashamed of being Max's lover.

She smiled pleasantly. "Good morning."

The girl hurried across the room to a small table beside the window. Francesca watched as she quickly set the table—for one, she suddenly realized, only for one.

But where was Max? Where was he?

"Signorina?"

The girl said something in her soft, musical voice. Francesca understood enough of the language now to know she was asking if she wanted anything else. She did; she wanted to know where Max was, but even if she could have phrased the question, she wouldn't have. How could you ask such a thing of a stranger on the first morning in your lover's bedroom?

"*Signorina?*"

Francesca swallowed. "Thank you," she said. "That's—that's all."

The maid smiled and stepped from the room, closing the door quietly after her. Francesca walked slowly to the table and poured a cup of coffee. She was making mountains out of molehills, that was what she was doing, looking for hidden meanings when there weren't any.

She took a sip of the coffee. Still, as soon as she saw Max, she was going to ask him to tell her, finally, why he'd brought her to Corsica. She wasn't a fool—she knew it had to have been part of some larger plan he'd devised to get even with Charles. That was behind them now, but she still needed to know the reason.

A tremor went through her. It *was* behind them, wasn't it?

She turned and made her way to the window, then settled into the window seat and stared out at the sea battling the rocks below. How different the view from this room was, compared to what you could see from hers. Her windows looked out on a gentle, quiet Sarcene, while Max's gave on to a Sarcene that was dark and untamed.

The cup trembled in her hand. She set it down carefully on the sill and took a deep breath.

Which was the real Sarcene, she thought suddenly, or were both illusions?

The castle was very quiet. Francesca's footsteps echoed eerily as she made her way down the stairs, then to the library. Perhaps Max was there.

But he wasn't. He wasn't anywhere, she knew that even before she'd finished searching for him. Giulia was in the kitchen; by now a mix of despair and anger had eroded her pride enough so that she felt no hesitancy in asking her the question she'd not asked the maid, but while she was working the words together in her head, trying to phrase it properly, the housekeeper said something she couldn't understand and hurried down the hall that led to the servants' quarters.

Francesca clamped her lips together. Damn you, Max, she thought. When I find you, I'm going to—I'm going to...

Her head came up. The stables. Of course. That's where he was. She strode from the kitchen, her pace increasing as she made her way to the front door. She pulled it open. Here she was, feeling sorry for herself, and all the time Max was——

"Buon giorno, signorina."

She blinked. As always, there was a polite, soft-spoken young man waiting for her just outside. It was either Paolo or Gianni or one of half a dozen other polite, soft-spoken young men, all of whom looked as if they were in training for body-building titles. Her irritation at being watched over constantly had kept her from separating one from another.

Francesca smiled wryly. Apparently, Max had forgotten to tell them that she was no longer under house arrest.

She nodded and said good morning, then started down the steps. Paolo or whoever he was fell in beside her.

"I'm going to the stables," she said pleasantly, motioning toward the outbuildings with a wave of her hand.

He smiled and kept stride with her.

She stopped and turned to face him. "You don't have to accompany me," she said carefully. "Do you understand?" She fixed her eyes on his face and shook her head from side to side. "I—don't—want—company."

She swung away and started walking; so did he.

Francesca spun toward him. "I don't need you with me," she insisted. *"Io—io no..."* Damn! She had no idea how to tell him that his presence was unnecessary. "The *signor* will explain, when you see him. He'll tell you that you don't have to watch me any more."

His smile never wavered. "I have already seen the *signor* this morning."

She stared at him in amazement. "You—you speak English?"

"I have seen him," he repeated, ignoring her question. "And he has instructed me to accompany you wherever you wish to go, *signorina*."

"No. You must have misunderstood. Things have changed."

Something flickered in the man's dark eyes. Pity, Francesca thought, it was pity.

"No, *signorina*, nothing has changed. Don Maximillian assured me of that. He told me that you might say such a thing, but he said it was not so. I am to stay with you, as I have from the beginning."

Everything seemed to stop. The early morning bird songs that had filled the air, the distant tinkle of bells, even the warm breeze that always swept up the slopes from the valley—all of it ceased while she looked into her guard's face, and then, stricken, she put her hand to her mouth and swung away from him.

God, oh God, it wasn't Paolo who'd misunderstood, it was she! She knew it with soul-wrenching certainty.

She had spent the night in Max's arms, but she was still the enemy. He had wanted her all along, he'd never made any pretense of it, and he'd finally done what he'd intended from the start, but with a technique so practiced that she'd become a willing participant instead of a pathetic victim.

What a fool she'd been. Everything—*everything*—that had happened was all part of an ugly scheme of revenge.

For one fierce moment, Francesca flamed with a rage so white-hot it made her gasp for air—and then, all too swiftly, the flame consumed itself and died. She was left with an ache so deep and piercing that she staggered back a step.

Paolo stepped forward and caught her elbow. "*Signorina*? Are you all right?"

Francesca wrenched free of his hand. "Don't touch me," she breathed. "Don't any of you touch me again."

She turned and ran for the house.

She waited in Max's room for his return, turning away the maid when she came to make the bed. She had thought it would be difficult, sitting in that place where she had given away all that she was, but in the end it had turned out to be the best decision she could have made. There was a bitter comfort in sitting here, her eyes on the rumpled bed that was an unfailing reminder of how she had been used. It gave her strength and chased the last bit of desire for Maximillian Donelli from her heart forever.

It was late by the time she heard his footsteps in the hall. She rose, switched on the lights, then peered into the mirror over the dresser. She looked fine, her hair sleekly drawn back from her face, her makeup perfect, her dress left carefully open from the hollow of her throat to the shadowed cleft between her breasts. Only her eyes, smudged with fatigue and pain, gave her away, but Max was hardly going to get the chance to gaze at her too closely.

She glanced across the room, to the table set with flowers and Waterford crystal, to the bottle of wine standing open. Her heart thudded. She was as ready as she would ever be.

The door swung open and Max entered the room. He looked worn and tired; for a breathless instant Francesca wanted to go to him and stroke the lines from his face. But then he shut the door and moved forward into the light. His eyes fastened on her, cold and hard, and she remembered that all that was left to her now was the swift victory of a first strike.

"Well," she said. Her tone was brisk. "You certainly stayed away long enough. Did you have a pleasant day?"

He leaned back against the closed door, arms crossed over his chest.

"What are you doing here, Francesca?"

She smiled brightly. "Waiting for you, naturally. What does it look like?"

His gaze moved beyond her, to the carefully set table, to the unmade bed.

"I am sorry I was not here when you awakened this morning. But I had to——"

"It doesn't matter." She smiled again. "I needed a day's rest anyway, after last night."

He stared at her, saying nothing, and then he headed away from the door and came slowly toward her.

"Francesca. We must talk."

"Talk?" She spun away from him toward where the opened bottle of wine waited, flashing a sultry smile over her shoulder. "Why would we talk, darling, when we do other things so much better?" She saw the look of surprise in his eyes and she turned her head away, praying he would not see her mouth tremble. "Shall I pour the wine now, or do you want to shower first? I'd offer to join you, but I spent the afternoon fixing my hair——"

"Francesca." His voice was very low. "Listen to me——"

"We can shower together later, though, after we've—after we've..."

Her lips started to form the ugly, harsh word but she couldn't say it. Max's face darkened with fury.

"Damn it to hell!" She winced as his hands bit down on her shoulders. "What is this game?" he demanded, spinning her to him.

"Game?" It took all her courage to lift her eyes to his. His angry expression and harsh stare almost stole her breath away, but she forced herself to go on. "I'm not playing games, Max. Not any more."

His eyes bored into hers. "And what is that supposed to mean?" Each word was hard as steel.

She shrugged lightly. "Come on, darling, don't make me spell it out."

Max's breath hissed between his teeth. "What the hell is going on? Stop this now, before I——"

Her smile was dazzling. "What I mean is, the act's over. You know—you, the masterful brigand, and me, the terrified innocent——"

His fingers carved into her flesh. "What are you saying?"

"You're hurting me." She swallowed. "Max. Did you hear what I said? You're hurting me."

She held her breath, waiting an eternity, and then he let go of her and brushed past her. Francesca cupped her shoulders in her hands, massaging the bruised flesh lightly, watching as he splashed wine into a glass, lifted it to his lips, and tossed it down.

"*Basta,*" he growled, slamming the empty glass on the table. "Enough of this, Francesca. If you have something to say, I suggest you say it."

Now was the time. All she had to do was take a deep breath, pin the bright, artificial, cocktail party smile to her face, and say the words she'd practiced the entire afternoon.

"Don't tell me you really thought..." She paused expectantly, brows arched, and then she laughed softly. "Oh, my. You did, didn't you? I thought—I never imagined——"

She caught her breath as he reached out for her. "What is this?" His voice was soft, ominous. "It's about what happened between us yesterday, isn't it?"

She hesitated, but she'd gone too far to stop now.

"Darling Max. I must say, I'm really flattered. The thing is, it was all—how shall I put it?—it was all a fantasy." She took a shallow breath in hopes it would slow her galloping heart. "Well, not quite all. I was quite serious at the beginning, when I said I'd never go to bed with you. I was very angry. You'd made me look so foolish at the Casino, and then there was the way you used me against Charles——"

"Charles? What has he to do with this?"

"Come on, Max. He has everything to do with it, and we both know it."

His eyes darkened. "Yes, of course. He is your stepbrother, and you would defend him against me with your last breath."

No, she thought, no, I wouldn't have. Not after you'd made love to me. For a little while, at least, the world had seemed clean, its colors fresh, and she had been certain, in her heart, that Max was not a man who would lie or steal—and that Charles, dear, sweet, weak Charles, might well be a man who could do both.

But that had been this morning. Now, knowing how Max had used her, she knew, too, that the only difference between him and her stepbrother was that while Charles might bend the rules out of fear of failure, Max would do it for the simple pleasure of getting what he wanted, and to hell with its effect on anyone else.

But he would not do it again. Not without remembering her.

Francesca stepped away from him and filled her glass with wine. "The point is," she said calmly, "that you changed the game when you kidnapped me." She smiled. "I was really furious."

"You were terrified." His voice was grim. "It took no great effort to see your fear, *cara*. So if you're going to try to pretend that you were not afraid——"

"Oh, I admit it. I was. But the fear was exhilarating, Max, and then, after you'd brought me here, to Sarcene." She threw out her arms, as if to embrace the room. "It was perfect. So—so medieval. That was when I knew."

"What?" he said, growling the word. "What did you know?"

"I knew," she said, despite the fear expanding in her chest, stealing her breath so that she could hardly breathe, "I knew that letting you seduce me would be electrifying."

Max moved closer to her. "I didn't seduce you, *cara*. I made love to you."

What was that darkness she saw in his eyes? Pain. No, it couldn't be pain. Hurt. Yes, he was hurt. She had wounded his pride, his arrogant Corsican pride.

"You know what I mean," she said, tossing her head. "These things always seem to follow a pattern. You meet somewhere, a man is interesting, you go back to his place or yours..." She swallowed and turned her back to him. "It's dull and boring, after a while. Some men do try to make things different. The Marqués, for instance——"

She cried out in pain as Max caught hold of her and spun her toward him.

"Are you telling me that what happened between us yesterday was all part of some little amusement for you?"

Francesca forced her eyes to meet his. "Of course. We both knew I'd give in eventually. It was just a matter of——"

"You're lying. You have never even been with another man. I could tell." His eyes narrowed at her smile. "Then—the things we did through the night, all those things you said were new to you—you have done them with other men?"

"Well, yes. Maybe not with as much enthusiasm, darling, I mean, you're very good at——"

Her head snapped back as his hand slammed across her face. "Bitch," he whispered. "Whore. Slut——"

Tears rose in her eyes and glistened on her lashes. "All this because you weren't the first, Max?" Her head lifted proudly. "Or is it because my little gambit outclassed yours?"

She waited, trembling. He was capable of anything—she could see the taut containment in his face, in the straining sinews in his neck. Finally, after a long, long time, he threw her from him.

"You and your stepbrother deserve each other," he said softly. "May the two of you burn in hell together."

She stared blindly after him as he turned and strode from the room. The door slammed shut and she stood silent, tears streaming down her face, and then she flung herself across the bed.

"Oh, God, Max," she whispered, "I loved you. I loved you so very much..."

You still love him, a voice inside her said tauntingly, and, even in the depths of her despair, Francesca knew it was the truth.

Eventually, her lashes fell to her cheeks and she fell into a deep, exhausted sleep. When she awoke, it was daylight and she knew, even before she stumbled from the room, that Max was gone.

There was no one in the castle except for Giulia, and somehow it came as no surprise to learn that she, too, spoke English.

"There is a car waiting for you," the housekeeper said coldly. "It will take you to the airport."

"Airport?" Francesca whispered.

Giulia smiled contemptuously. "Did you really think Corsicans are so provincial, *signorina*?"

Francesca turned away and closed her eyes. What she thought no longer mattered. She had given her heart to Max Donelli, and he had broken it.

What could possibly matter more than that?

The answer came thirty thousand feet over the Atlantic, when she placed a call to Charles, in New York. The sound of her voice sent him into a rage.

"Goddamn it," he snarled, "have you lost your mind? Where are you?"

"On my way home," she said, rubbing the bridge of her nose wearily. "I know you've been worried——"

"Worried?" He gave a bark of laughter. "Why would I worry? Hell, there's nothing to worry about any more."

"Charles, please. When I see you——"

"When you see me," he said bitterly, "you can explain how your boyfriend hypnotized you into missing the stockholders' meeting."

"The stockholders..." Francesca puffed out her breath. "I'm sorry, Charles, I guess I forgot. I'm sure no one noticed I wasn't——"

"Donelli threw me out," he said, his voice raw with anguish.

"What are you talking about? How could he? We have the controlling stock."

"Yes. We. *We*, do you understand? Without you here to vote your shares——"

Suddenly, it all made terrible sense. Her head fell back against the seat. Charles's voice droned hoarsely in her ear, explaining that Max had quietly bought large blocks of Spencer stock over the past months, that he had put in an unexpected appearance at the meeting, that, without her votes to stop him, he had wrested control from Charles.

But her stepbrother's explanation was unnecessary. Everything had suddenly fallen into place. Francesca understood why Max had carried her off to Corsica, why he'd kept her at Sarcene—and why he'd abandoned her so easily, and so coldly, today.

Maximillian Donelli had had two goals—to destroy Charles, and to seduce her—and he had accomplished both.

CHAPTER TWELVE

CHARLES SPENCER frowned, shoved back his chair, and stalked to the window. Fifty storeys below his penthouse apartment, people scurried like ants along the icy January streets of New York City.

Francesca, seated on the black kidskin sofa that faced the dazzling wall of glass, sighed in weary anticipation. She was fairly certain that she knew what he was going to say even before he said it.

He didn't disappoint her. "I hate this damned city in winter," he said gruffly. "We were in Palm Springs this time last year, remember? Hell, that's where we should be now."

He'd made the same speech, or variations on it, endless times during the past six months. Since being ousted from his position at Spencer's, Charles had seized every opportunity to make it sound as if they were living on the edge of poverty when the simple truth was that the shares of stock he and Francesca owned in the company were paying more handsomely than ever. Max Donelli was the chairman of the board of directors and he had put his own man in as CEO. The firm was doing extraordinarily well.

"Brilliant," was how the *Wall Street Journal* described the takeover.

"Innovative," said the *Times*'s financial analyst.

But Charles was given to more colorful descriptions of Donelli, and he was starting on them now, as he stared out of the window.

"That SOB changed our lives," he said angrily. "That no-good bastard——"

"Charles, for heaven's sake." Francesca rose and walked to his side. "We've all the money we could

173

possibly want," she said, putting her hand on his shoulder. "Why must you keep torturing yourself?"

Her stepbrother swung his head toward her. "Money," he said grimly, "is not everything. I can't show my face anywhere without seeing people's eyebrows lift into their hairlines. You don't know——"

"Don't I? People have had a field day, speculating about what happened when I was on Corsica with him." Her voice turned bitter. "I'm the woman who Max Donelli walked out on, and you're the man he tossed off Spencer's board."

"What *did* go on when you were in Corsica?" Charles looked at her. "You've never really told me."

No. She hadn't. She'd admitted she'd been with Max the night of the Marqués's party, but she'd refused to tell Charles anything but the most inconsequential details about the time she'd spent at Sarcene. What had happened there was too demeaning and personal to talk about. It was an agony to remember it.

"Francesca?"

"Nothing went on. I mean, I've told you. He kept me under lock and key, that's all."

"The impudent SOB! He thinks he's so clever. He knows we can't afford to bring charges against him."

She nodded. They had been all through this. Bringing charges would have only made matters worse. What would she have said, in a court of law? That she had willingly become her kidnapper's lover?

Charles didn't know that, of course; his reasoning was that they couldn't bring charges against Max because of the publicity. Max had warned her that was what her stepbrother would say, she thought suddenly.

"...destroyed us, damn him!"

She drew a deep breath. "I—I'm sorry, Charles. What did you say?"

"I said, the son of a bitch damned near destroyed us."

"Yes." Her voice was soft. "Yes, he did."

"At least *I* figured him right. How the bastard took you in——"

"We've been all through this," she said. "I've told you, I don't want to discuss it."

"When I think of the men you've been cold to——"

"Dammit, didn't you hear me? I don't——"

"The Marqués himself, for God's sake! If you'd stayed with him that night, where you belonged . . ."

"Where I belonged?" she said softly. "Just what's that supposed to mean?"

"Nothing. Only that—that he was our host. And he liked you."

"He made my skin crawl."

"But Donelli didn't." His lips curled with distaste. "A man who made his money hauling fish, for God's sake."

"What do you mean?"

"Exactly what I said. He started with a broken-down fishing boat in Corsica and ended up with a fleet of cargo ships."

"I thought he owned a financial firm that competed with Spencer's."

"Among a dozen other things. That's why it's so ludicrous that he should have gotten so touchy over a little misunderstanding. Just because I instituted some strategies that may have been similar to his——"

Her head lifted. "You said that the strategies you'd introduced at Spencer's were your own, that you'd developed them."

Color spread across her stepbrother's cheekbones. "I did. I simply meant that Donelli had similar plans in his computer bank."

Francesca's gaze swept across his face. "But how would you know that, Charles?"

"How would I . . . ?" His tongue snaked out of his mouth and touched the corners of his lips. "He—er—he said so, remember? He—er—he accused me of tapping into his system."

Everything went very still. "But you didn't," she said softly.

"How can you ask such a question? No, of course I didn't. I wouldn't know how, just for openers."

"Through an employee. That was what Max said. He said you'd used someone who worked for him to——"

"I don't know any of Donelli's employees. How would I?"

"I'm just telling you what he said, Charles. He said——"

"I know what he said." His mouth narrowed. "And I'm stunned that you'd have even listened to such lies about me. You and I have always been so close——"

Francesca closed her eyes. "I'm sorry."

"I practically raised you, Francesca, and now this—this barbarian comes along and you'd rather believe him than me."

"Please." She put her arms around him and kissed his cheek. "I apologize, Charles. I've just—I've been working too hard, I suppose. I'm just edgy."

She felt the tension drain from his body. "That's because you insist on doing things foolishly," he said, slipping his arm around her waist as they strolled to the door. "Honestly, darling, I don't know what's got into you. Working extra hours at that silly gallery, moving out of here into that little apartment in the village——"

She laughed. "You make it sound like a life of deprivation, and you know it's not. It's just that it's time I grew up and stood on my own feet."

"I hardly see you any more." They stopped at the door and he turned her toward him. "Do you realize that it's months since you've gone anywhere with me?"

Francesca's smile wavered. "Meaning I haven't accompanied you on the usual winter circuit. The dinners, the theater, the opera..."

"Yes." Charles was still smiling, but there was a tightness to his mouth. "Yes, that's right. People keep saying, where's that lovely sister of yours, Spencer?"

"Tell them she has better things to do than stand around chatting about the charity of the moment," she said with forced lightness.

"Refusing to face our friends won't make the gossip go away, darling."

"They're not our friends. Not mine, anyway. You know how I feel about that whole scene." She sighed. "You're right about the gossip, I suppose. And I know the only way to shut people up would be to show myself. But——"

"Exactly. I'm glad you agree."

"...but I can't. The very thought of——"

Her stepbrother's hands kneaded her shoulders. "I'd be at your side, darling, for moral support."

"No, I couldn't."

"Are you going to hide for the rest of your life because that bastard made fools of us?" He clasped her head between his palms and looked into her eyes. "What if I told you I'd found a way to return the favor?"

"Get back your position at Spencer's, you mean? But how? Max has all the votes he needs. Everyone's delighted with the way the company's been operating."

"Only because they're fools," Charles said harshly. "Donelli tells lies, and people believe them."

"Yes." Her voice was very soft. "He's good at that."

"Don't I know it?" He let go of her and strode across the room to the drinks trolley. "Just look at the things he told you about me. That I'd stolen his research, his client list..." Ice cubes clattered as he dumped a handful into a crystal tumbler. "Want one?" he asked, holding out a bottle of Scotch.

Francesca shook her head. "Tell me what you meant just now. How will you oust Max Donelli from Spencer's? Did you find a way to buy up shares?"

"That wouldn't work. Besides, it's too expensive now. I'm not interested in dumping the bastard, Francesca. What I want is to nail his . . ." He smiled coldly. "I want to do to him what he's done to me."

"To us, you mean."

"Of course." Charles gulped a mouthful of Scotch. "I want to destroy him, once and for all."

Her mouth went dry. "Destroy him?"

"Yes."

"But how?"

He smiled tightly. "You'll see, darling." He lifted his glass to his lips and drank off the remaining pale gold liquid in one swallow. "In fact, if you're a good girl, I may just let you be part of Donelli's downfall. How would you like that?"

Would she like that? Would she like the chance to ruin Maximillian Donelli, to double the pain that he'd caused her?

Francesca's throat tightened. People said that hate was the other side of love, but she'd never believed it until that terrible day at Sarcene, when she'd seen Max for what he really was. His was the face she saw when she awakened, the face she saw before she fell asleep. Her days were filled with him; she saw him in every tall, dark-haired male striding along the street.

She kept telling Charles to put what had happened behind him, but the truth was she hadn't managed to take her own advice. Max's name and face never left her mind. She despised him, and if sometimes her heart ached in the remembering, if sometimes she awoke with her cheeks damp with tears——

"Francesca?" She looked up. Charles was standing in front of her, watching her with a strange look on his face. "You don't—you can't possibly have any feelings for the man, can you?"

She drew back her shoulders. "Tell me what you want. I'll do anything."

Charles smiled, leaned forward, and kissed her forehead. "I promise you," he said, "by this time next week, we'll be toasting the spectacular demise of Maximillian Donelli."

Standing in the elaborate powder room of the Plaza Hotel, Francesca thought for what seemed the one hundredth time that she had been a fool to accompany Charles tonight. But he'd held out bait too enticing to refuse when he'd telephoned.

"This is it," he'd said mysteriously. "I've worked out the perfect scheme to topple that bastard."

He'd refused to say anything else, telling her only that she was to wear her best dress, promising he'd tell her the details when he picked her up at her apartment. But he hadn't, he'd simply whisked her off to this hotel.

Their limousine had pulled to the curb. Charles, in his impatience, had opened the door himself—something he never did—stepped onto the pavement, and held out his hand to her.

"Well, come on, come on. We're late."

Francesca had felt a moment's panic. Charles was so excited and eager. What was his scheme to cripple Max?

"Charles—wait. You have to tell me——"

He'd tugged her hand hard enough to half drag her from the car.

"Didn't you hear me, Francesca? We're late. I told Gerry we'd be here by eight, and it's half past that already."

"Gerry? Gerry who?"

Now, looking at herself in the mirror, Francesca grimaced. "Gerry" had turned out to be Gerald Watley, sixtyish, married, and a longtime member of Spencer's board of directors. She had never liked the man, especially since he'd tried to paw her at a Christmas party two years before. Charles had always treated him with disdain—but tonight, he'd acted as if Watley were his long-lost brother.

The powder room door swung open, admitting a blast of music from the ballroom along with a trio of chattering women. All three stopped dead when they saw Francesca, then rushed toward her in a swoop.

"Darling! How good to see you. You've been out of circulation for ages. How have you been?"

She gave them a frozen smile, avoided saying anything more than what politeness demanded, and made a hurried exit—straight into Gerald Watley.

He caught her by the shoulders and laughed good-naturedly as she collided with him.

"Ah, Miss Drury. Charles sent me to find you. They'll be serving dinner soon, and we haven't even had our first dance."

Francesca peered past him as he led her into the ballroom. "Where is my stepbrother, Mr. Watley?"

Watley's arms closed around her. "Please call me Gerry, Francesca."

She stiffened as he tried to draw her closer. He was perspiring—she could see beads of moisture on his shiny face and in his sparse moustache—and he smelled unpleasantly of too much expensive cologne.

"Did Charles say which table he and I are at? I didn't pick up my seating card——"

"You're with me, of course." He swung her past the bandstand, his voice rising as the music blared. "You needn't worry about Charles, my dear. You're in good hands."

Good hands, indeed. One of those hands was on her bare back, clammy and moist.

"Mr. Watley——"

"Gerry, darling. Call me Gerry."

"Mr. Watley." She smiled through her teeth. Where was Charles, damn him? "I can hardly breathe, the way you're holding me."

Watley chuckled. "That's such a charming quality you have, Francesca, I've always been fascinated by it. That don't-touch-me thing, you know what I mean? That's why I was especially delighted when your stepbrother phoned and told me that you'd mentioned my name."

She blinked. "That I'd—I'd mentioned your name?"

"I'd no idea my interest in you was reciprocated, my dear."

She felt herself pale. "Mr. Watley. I think you misunderstood whatever my stepbrother may have told you. I——"

She caught her breath as his hand slipped, just for a second, to the small of her back.

"My wife's away." There was a hoarseness in his voice. "Although you needn't worry. She and I have an understanding about these things. I thought we'd have supper here, then go on to a little club I know in the Village, and then——"

Her hands rose between them to push his hulking body from her, and then she stiffened. Someone was watching her, she could feel it, feel his eyes on her.

It was Max, she knew it even before she looked over Watley's shoulder and saw him. There he was, on the far side of the dance floor. There was a woman in his arms, a beautiful woman, and her face was turned up to his, her smile was meant for him alone—but Max wasn't paying any attention. His eyes were fixed on Francesca, he was watching her as if the planet had been reduced to the size of this one ballroom and she and he were the only man and woman on it.

Francesca's breath caught. This was how it had been that first night, the same stunning sense of destiny, the same heightened awareness, and in that instant, she knew that she would never stop loving him.

Her throat worked. She mouthed his name or perhaps whispered it, and Gerald Watley pulled her tightly into his arms so that her hands, which were lying flat against his chest, slid up to his shoulders. The look of derision on Max's face was the last thing she saw before the crowd surged between them.

Watley made a little humming sound. "That's the look I want to see on your face, darling," he whispered thickly, his breath warm and fetid on her face. "That look that says you can't wait to have me touch you——"

He grunted as she trod down deliberately on his foot, her high-heeled sandal bearing sharply into his instep.

"Hey. Hey, what are you——?"

"I suggest you let go of me," she said quietly, "or it will be my knee you feel next."

Watley's arms fell to his sides as she stepped away from him. She turned, head high, and made her way across the crowded dance floor, ignoring the "hello's and the raised eyebrows. She was trembling by the time she reached the cloakroom, eager only for a quick exit— but Charles, damn him, had the claim tag for her velvet evening cape in his pocket.

She stepped up to the cloakroom window.

"I haven't got the tag," she told the attendant, "but I must leave here. I——" A hand closed on her arm; she whirled around and found herself face-to-face with her stepbrother.

"What in hell are you doing?" he said through his teeth.

"Let go of me, Charles."

"Francesca. I asked you a question." He clamped his lips together, glared at the attendant, and then his hand tightened on her and he half dragged her toward a bank of low couches separated from the rest of the foyer by an oriental folding screen.

"I have nothing to say to you, Charles," she hissed. "Just let go of me."

"How dare you?" He tugged her down on to a seat beside him, his face white with rage. "How dare you ruin everything, after all the trouble I went to to set it up?"

Francesca twisted away. "Set it up?" She rubbed furiously at the marks his fingers had left on her arm. "Set *me* up, you mean. What in heaven did you promise that man, anyway?"

Charles's mouth thinned. "Why must you always be such a child about these things, Francesca? Watley's an important man."

"He's a pig, and you used to think so, too."

"He's important to my plan, dammit. I told you I'd figured a way to finish Donelli off." He thrust his hand into his hair and scraped it back from his forehead. "Look, it's not too late. Watley's confused, but I assured him you were just playing hard to get. That's the reputation you have. He'll buy it, if you go back in there and treat him nicely."

A coldness settled around her heart. "Treat him nicely?" she said softly. "The way you wanted me to treat the Marqués, you mean?"

Her stepbrother's eyes slid from hers. "Don't make it sound like that."

"Like what? Like—like whoring?"

His jaw thrust forward. "I've tried and tried to explain, but you just refuse to listen. You're an asset, Francesca, and there's nothing wrong in making the most of an asset."

"What's tonight's plan, Charles? Am I to learn something from Watley?"

Her stepbrother relaxed a little. "What could you possibly learn from a stupid fool like Gerry Watley?" he said, with a contemptuous curl to his mouth. He edged closer. "You have it backward, darling. He's to learn something from you. You're to drop some information to him, casually, when—well, when you and he are alone and relaxed."

It felt as if there were a knot in her belly. "Pillow talk," she said quietly, watching him. "Is that what you mean?"

Charles flushed. "I worked hard at this scheme, Francesca. Do you want to hear me out, or don't you?"

She didn't. Suddenly, she didn't want to hear anything from her stepbrother—but she knew she had to, just as she knew she had to ask him questions that he'd already answered but which she now suspected needed asking—and answering—again.

"All right." Her voice was very quiet and controlled. "Tell me your plan."

He smiled. "It's simple, darling. I'll tell you some things about our friend Mr. Donelli, and you'll pass them on to Watley."

"What things?"

Her stepbrother shrugged his shoulders. "Things, that's all, nothing to worry your pretty head about. Just bits and pieces about a conversation you'll claim you overheard at the gallery the other day, someone saying that Donelli's going to swallow Spencer's."

Francesca stared at him. "Is that true?"

"Dammit, Francesca, you aren't listening! No, it's not true. But you'll make it sound as if it is. Everyone who's anyone passes through that gallery where you work. You don't have to name names, just hint that it was somebody important, that you've heard that Donelli plans to dump Spencer's current board of directors and put his own people in it. That's all Watley needs to hear. He'll contact the others, they'll turn on Donelli so fast it will make his head spin, and——"

"But if none of it's true, Charles—I can't do it. I can't just lie that way."

She gasped as his hands clamped on to hers. "Little Miss Sunshine," he snarled. "What do you prefer? That this—this barbarian make a fool of me and get away with it?"

"No. Of course not. But——"

"You said you'd do anything. Well, I'm telling you what it is you have to do and now you're trying to back out."

"Charles, please listen. Max Donelli hurt me, too. He humiliated both of us."

His face twisted. "You don't know the meaning of the word. You owe me this, dammit."

Francesca looked at him. "Owe you? What's that supposed to mean?"

"If it weren't for you, none of this would have happened."

She flushed. "I wasn't the one who made that awful wager."

Charles leaned toward her, his face a hideous mask of rage. "If my dear father hadn't been such an ass——"

"What?"

"If he had left me all the shares he owned, do you think I'd be in this mess?" Spittle formed at the corners of his mouth. "Who in hell were you? You weren't even a blood relation, Francesca, you were just a—a waif he picked up along with your mother. But he was won over by that saccharine sweetness of yours, he left you half of what should have been mine."

Her face turned white. "You don't know what you're saying."

"Donelli's administrative assistant had the same, sweet 'I can't be touched' attitude, too, when I first met her. But I turned her on to the real world. She got me into his computer files, she got me everything I needed."

"Max was right," Francesca whispered. "You did steal from him."

Charles let go of her hands. "I did what I had to for Spencer's, that's all. If you'd ever had the responsibilities I've had, you'd understand."

"Oh, God." Francesca buried her face in her hands. "I should have known he wouldn't have lied to me. Not Max. Not—— "

"Please, you're making me sick. What did the son of a bitch do, hypnotize you?"

Her hands fell to her lap. "He showed me what a real man can be," she said softly. "He showed me that a man can be honest and strong and caring and——"

"Honest? He kidnapped you. How honest was that?"

"He thought I was part of your scheme, Charles. He thought——" Her voice broke. "He thought I was all the things you'd tried to make me, a woman who slept around, who used men for her own purposes—and I— I made sure he believed it, I..." She puffed out her breath. "That last day, he said we had to talk. He wanted me to listen, but——"

Charles slammed his hand on the couch in disgust. "God. To hear you talk, you'd think you were in love with the son of a—— "

"Yes. That is what one might think, *cara*. That you were in love with Max Donelli."

She flew up from the couch as Max stepped out slowly from behind the folding screens. Her hand went to her throat.

"Max. How long have you——?"

"Long enough." His eyes, as dark as the night, lingered on her flushed face and he smiled just a little before looking down at Charles, still seated on the couch, his skin the color of ashes. "Spencer," he said softly.

Charles gulped and got to his feet. "I'll deny everything," he stammered. "Whatever you think you heard——"

"What you will do," Max said, "is sell your shares in Spencer's to me tomorrow morning. I will pay you today's closing price—plus five percent."

Charles's brows rose. "Five percent?"

"Yes." Max took a step forward. "If that doesn't suit you, we can step outside and discuss the matter man-to-man."

"No," Charles said quickly, "no, that's—that's fine. I—I——"

"Good night, Spencer."

Francesca put out her hand. "Charles?" Tears filled her eyes as her stepbrother brushed past her and walked away. "Charles," she said again, and suddenly she was in Max's arms.

"It's all right, *cara*," he whispered. "Cry, if you must."

"I never knew he felt that way about me. He—he did things, and said things, but—but I wanted to believe him. He was my big brother..."

Max's hands cupped her head and brought it to his shoulder. "He was a fool," he said sharply. "Any man would be, to try and use you so."

She drew back a little. "I'm ruining your dinner jacket," she said with a hesitant smile.

"Francesca." Max took her face in his hands and lifted it to him. "God, how I've missed you."

She sniffed back her tears. "You don't have to say that, Max. I know why you did the things you did. You thought I was——"

"I thought you were a woman who would steal my heart, *cara*." He smiled. "And I was right."

She was afraid to breathe for fear of destroying the magic weaving around them.

"I don't—I don't understand," she whispered.

Max bent his head and kissed her tenderly. "I love you, Francesca," he said. "That was what I wanted to tell you that last night."

Her hands lifted to his chest. "Oh, Max——"

"I wanted to tell you everything." His voice grew fierce. "All of it, that I'd stolen you away to keep you from voting your stock in your stepbrother's favor——"

"You mean, you knew, that night at the Casino, that there was a Spencer's stockholders' meeting scheduled?"

Max shook his head. "I never even thought of it until we were en route to Villefranche. And then the idea began to come together. I telephoned *Moondrift* to arrange for our dinner—and to have a call placed to New York, to verify the date of the meeting." He sighed deeply. "The answer arrived by cable, just as you and I were finishing our meal."

Francesca leaned back in his arms. "Then—then you didn't kidnap me because you wanted me?"

He smiled and kissed her again, a long, lingering kiss that left her breathless.

"I kept telling myself I'd taken you to destroy Charles."

"A gambit," she said softly.

Max nodded. "But every time I looked at you, *cara*, my heart told me the truth. I had taken you because I wanted you, because I'd never known a woman like you in my life."

Her hands rose to his shoulders. "But—but that last day, Max. After all we'd shared——"

"*Cara*. If I could only erase what happened——"

"I could have gotten away that day we went riding. You must have realized that. But I didn't. I chose to stay with you. I was so desperately in love with you."

Max kissed her. "Was?" he asked softly.

"Am," she said, smiling. "I am in love with you, Max Donelli. I only said those things to hurt you because *I* was so hurt." She smiled a little sadly. "You'd read my mind so many times before—if only you'd read it then, you'd have known my heart was breaking. When I awoke and found you gone, when you didn't come back——" She drew a shaky breath. "When I found I was still under guard, that nothing had changed——"

"*Cara*, how can I explain?" Max took her hands from his shoulders and kissed the palms. "I awoke with you in my arms that morning, and I knew there was no point in trying to kid myself any longer. I'd fallen in love with you and I had to tell you that I'd carried you off to ruin your stepbrother." He put her hands against his chest. "I looked at your beautiful face and I didn't know what to do. Nothing had changed—and everything had changed. How could I tell you? What would you say?"

"And so you decided not to tell me anything?"

"No," he said quickly. "No, I knew I must. But I needed to think. So I went off, alone. It was stupid, I know that now. But I am not used to sharing myself, *cara*. Can you see? There's never been anyone in my life or in my heart."

Francesca rose on her toes and kissed his mouth. When she drew back, she was smiling.

"Nor in mine," she said. "You were the first man I ever loved, Max, the first I ever made love with."

"And the last," he said in that gruff, proud way she knew so well.

She laughed softly. "Oh, yes," she whispered, "there's no question about that."

"Francesca." Max let go of her and took a step back. Slowly, smiling into her eyes, he held his hands out to her. "Will you come with me, if I ask?"

Her heart lifted. "Yes," she said simply. "I will."

She put her hand in his and his fingers clasped hers tightly.

"And will you marry me, *cara*, and love me forever?"

"Forever," Francesca said, and Max gathered her into his arms and kissed her and kissed her until the world spun around them, and all at once she could smell the wildflowers of Sarcene in the air.

POSTCARDS FROM EUROPE

HARLEQUIN PRESENTS®

Travel across Europe in 1994 with Harlequin Presents. Collect a new <u>Postcards From Europe</u> title each month!

Don't miss
DARK SUNLIGHT
by Patricia Wilson
Harlequin Presents #1644

Available in April, wherever Harlequin Presents books are sold.

HPPFE4

Hi—

The sun was shining brightly here in Spain <u>until</u> I met Felipe de Santis. The man is used to giving orders and doesn't respect my abilities as a journalist. But I'm going to get my story—and I'm going to help Felipe's sister!

Love, Maggie

P.S. If only I could win Felipe's love....

Take 4 bestselling love stories FREE

Plus get a FREE surprise gift!

Special Limited-time Offer

Mail to Harlequin Reader Service®

3010 Walden Avenue
P.O. Box 1867
Buffalo, N.Y. 14269-1867

YES! Please send me 4 free Harlequin Presents® novels and my free surprise gift. Then send me 6 brand-new novels every month, which I will receive months before they appear in bookstores. Bill me at the low price of $2.44 each plus 25¢ delivery and applicable sales tax, if any*. That's the complete price and—compared to the cover prices of $2.99 each—quite a bargain! I understand that accepting the books and gift places me under no obligation ever to buy any books. I can always return a shipment and cancel at any time. Even if I never buy another book from Harlequin, the 4 free books and the surprise gift are mine to keep forever.

106 BPA ANRH

Name	(PLEASE PRINT)
Address	Apt. No.
City	State	Zip

This offer is limited to one order per household and not valid to present Harlequin Presents® subscribers. *Terms and prices are subject to change without notice. Sales tax applicable in N.Y.

UPRES-94R   ©1990 Harlequin Enterprises Limited

Meet Kieran Sinclair. He believes Tegan heartlessly jilted his wheelchair-bound friend and now he's determined to exact revenge—in the form of her pagan surrender.

And then there's Jerome Moncourt. When Meg accidentally falls into his arms, she discovers that she isn't the only one participating in a dangerous charade. The handsome Frenchman has his own secrets!

Kieran and Jerome are just two of the sexy men you'll fall in love with each month in Harlequin Presents Plus.

Watch for
Pagan Surrender by Robyn Donald
Harlequin Presents Plus #1639

and

Dawn Song by Sara Craven
Harlequin Presents Plus #1640

Harlequin Presents Plus
The best has just gotten better!

Available in April, wherever Harlequin books are sold.

PPLUS11